S0-BZY-406

THE NOOSE'S SHADOW

Master Mercurius Mysteries
Book Four

Graham Brack

SAPERE
BOOKS

THE NOOSE'S
SHADOW

Published by Sapere Books.

20 Windermere Drive, Leeds, England, LS17 7UZ,
United Kingdom

saperebooks.com

Copyright © Graham Brack, 2020

Graham Brack has asserted his right to be identified as the
author of this work.

All rights reserved.

No part of this publication may be reproduced, stored in any
retrieval system, or transmitted, in any form, or by any means,
electronic, mechanical, photocopying, recording, or otherwise,
without the prior written permission of the publishers.

This book is a work of fiction. Names, characters, businesses,
organisations, places and events, other than those clearly in the
public domain, are either the product of the author's
imagination, or are used fictitiously.

Any resemblances to actual persons, living or dead, events or
locales are purely coincidental.

ISBN: 978-1-80055-137-4

PROLOGUE

My room is cold in winter. It has always been so, but now that I am over eighty years old, I feel it all the more keenly. My clerk, Jan van der Meer, is very good at keeping the fire going, but then he has an interest in not freezing as he writes at my dictation.

The University of Leiden, which God preserve, has not yet required me to retire. There are two reasons for this, I think. First, when the Statutes were first created the idea that any of the professors might live into old age did not seem to occur to anyone. They may have been right; a list of University teaching staff shows that many died in their prime. The second is that I am now paid per lecture and I do not teach much, so I do not cost them much either. My room and board substitute for a pension, and both sides seem content with this arrangement.

I supplement my income with the sale of these little fragments from my journals, out of which I pay Van der Meer a disproportionate amount for the mere act of spelling the words correctly, which he manages most of the time.

I was fortunate in that my work for great men brought rewards which kept body and soul together. More importantly, they sometimes allowed me to work pro bono for those who could not have afforded to pay. And the story I am about to tell is one of those.

Now and again, well-meaning readers take the trouble to tell me that I have erred in my recollection because such and such a building had fallen down by the time I describe, or I've got the name of somebody's wife wrong. To which I ask how they know that? Surely because they have read somebody else's recollection which is just as likely to be faulty as mine, if not more so, because I have an excellent memory.

Bear in mind also that I may have changed one or two things to protect those I knew who are still alive, if any of them are, which I doubt.

Anyway, these are my memoirs. If you don't like them, write your own.

Leiden, St Tiburtius' Day, 1720.

CHAPTER ONE

I was lingering after supper in the refectory, earning myself some scowls from Albrecht the kitchen master, who wanted to close up and go to bed. Well, who was stopping him? It was the fact that this was the warmest place in the building that bleak January day that was keeping me there; certainly not the hope of any more of what he optimistically called "cooking". If I were a self-respecting pig, I would understand that my purpose in life was to be taken one day to have my throat cut and my flesh consumed by appreciative humans; and I would take great care that I should not fall into the hands of Albrecht, who did for the culinary art what the Vandals did for interior design in Rome.

His wife, Mechtild, on the other hand, is an angel in human form. Not, perhaps, as beautiful as one of Rubens' angels, but then they probably don't have Mechtild's touch with pastry. Her cheese flan is just the sort of food that angels would be fed, if they ever had to eat. Opinion is divided on that point. Being immortal, angels cannot require sustenance; but then Psalm seventy-seven, verse twenty-five, tells us *"Panem angelorum manducavit homo"* or, as I would translate it, "men ate the bread of angels", which demonstrates that even if they do not need food, they have it.

'Do you require anything else, Master?' Mechtild asked.

'No, thank you, Mechtild; please close up as usual. I'll just sit here enjoying the warmth and finish my ale. But don't let me keep you.'

Mechtild smiled and lifted my tankard to give the table a swift cleaning. 'Shall I top that up for you, Master?'

'Why not? Thank you, Mechtild.'

She took it away and returned with a tankard full to the brim and a small cloth. 'When you've finished, sir, perhaps you'd wipe the tankard round with the cloth and leave it on the side table there.'

'Of course.'

She waddled off to bed and I unfolded the cloth which, as I expected, contained a couple of biscuits. My own mother had died some years before, but if I had been looking for a replacement then Mechtild would have done very well. Mulling this over, I realised that she was probably not much older than I was. In that January of 1680 I was forty-one years old, still unmarried (to the disgust of my grandmother, who had given up waiting and died the previous autumn) and likely always to be so because I was an ordained Roman Catholic priest.

I had been a Protestant minister first, of course, or I doubt they would have allowed me anywhere near the Faculty of Theology, but in 1664 I was ordained a priest in France, with strict instructions to keep my faith to myself so that if there were another round of persecutions, the Church in the United Provinces would have some replacement priests to keep the flame burning. Not, perhaps, the best choice of metaphor there, given the preferred method of disposing of Catholic priests, but no matter.

If you have read the previous small volumes of my memoirs, you may recall that after single-handedly rescuing the marriage negotiations between William, Prince of Orange and Princess Mary of England, I came home to some carping criticism from the Rector of the University, Johannes Coccius, who had belatedly realised that I did not have a doctorate and proposed to demote me to the Artes faculty unless I acquired one. The Artes is a sort of kindergarten level for students, which all are required to complete before they enter the higher Faculties of Law, Medicine or Theology or, more often, go home to earn a living and escape their debts, and I had no wish to teach there because I had seen those students at close quarters and many of them were unteachable. There were some whose intellect was such that you marvelled that their mothers had ever managed to toilet-train them.

Anyway, remembering that William was Most Supreme Governor of the University, and that he had once said if he could ever do anything for me I only had to ask, I decided to put this to the test by asking him for an honorary doctorate. To my surprise, a couple of weeks later I was summoned to the Rector's office to ask what I was playing at.

'I'm sorry, Rector, I don't understand,' I said.

Coccius waved a letter at me. 'This! The Stadhouder orders the University to give you an honorary doctorate. For what?'

'Services rendered, I suppose, Rector. Though I am not at liberty to describe them.'

'I can hardly stand in front of everyone at a graduation and announce that "We're giving Mercurius an honorary doctorate but I can't tell you what for", can I?'

'I suppose not,' I agreed. 'Can we say "Personal services to the Stadhouder"?'

'It makes you sound like his valet.'

'Services to the State?'

'That suggests that you are a spy. You're not, are you?' he asked.

'I'm not suited to subterfuge,' I answered, which I allow was a bit rich since I had triggered all this by asking for a degree behind his back.

'Well, we can hardly refuse a request from the Stadhouder, but you need to furnish me with an acceptable reason. I thought you were taking a doctorate anyway?'

This was a reference to his plan to get Professor Spanheim to provide me with a supervisor for a doctorate earned in the normal way. It was just that while the University regulations undoubtedly said that lecturing staff in the higher faculties must have doctorates, nowhere could I find that it said that they had to be earned.

I was not averse to doing the work, nor did I doubt my capacity to complete a doctorate. Goodness, when you looked at some of the people we have graduated in my time at Leiden, you'd think that all you had to do to get one was write your name legibly at the top of a sheet of paper. No, it was more to do with Spanheim's attempts to impose a rigid Calvinism on all our work. Spanheim liked an argument, and in his time he had started one with almost everyone. He spoke out against Arminians, Cartesians (especially Cartesians) and Catholics alike and was a committed proponent of double predestinationism. We need not dwell on that; all the reader needs to know is that Spanheim believed that only a select few were going to get to Heaven, and, to be honest, if it is filled with people like Spanheim I'm not sure that I'd want to go anyway.

Two things happened to derail Coccius' little plan. First, Spanheim declared that he had insufficient time to supervise me and handed me over to Christoph Wittich instead, who was much more congenial to me. Second, Coccius dropped dead. I bear the man no ill will, and I was delighted to note that at his funeral we were all in our full academic dress, which proved that we had all read his memorandum on the subject. He would have liked that.

As a result of this, there was a pleasant little ceremony at which I was awarded the title of Doctor honoris causa. This meant that I now fulfilled the requirements of the University to remain in the Faculty of Theology without the need to do any work that I did not want to do. I could not use the title, of course, hence Mechtild calling me Master, but that did not matter one whit; and, if all went according to plan, I should soon earn my real doctorate. Now that I no longer had to do it, I was feeling quite keen on the idea. The new Rector, Charles Drelincourt, was a French physician who had better things to worry about than whether a lowly lecturer in moral philosophy had the right bits of parchment on his wall.

I could hear hailstones slapping against the windows and was feeling very glad that I had no reason to go out that night when I heard a rapping at the door. This puzzled me, because the door should still have been unlocked at that time so that students could return, and I was even more intrigued when I heard a woman's voice as she spoke with one of the porters. I could not hear what was being said, but after a while I heard the door close, and, shortly afterwards, the porter poked his head around the door of the refectory and walked towards me once he had identified the fur-wrapped bundle by the fire as me.

'I thought you might be here, Master,' he announced.

'I certainly wouldn't go out, tempting though the inn on the Langebrug is.'

'There's a woman here asking for you,' he said.

'Here? At this time?'

'Yes, Master.'

'I don't think I know any women,' I said.

Of course, this was not strictly true. I know quite a few women but none who would brave a freezing January night to see me. Even my late mother would probably have sent a boy with a note telling me to come to her.

'Well, she seems to know you, sir. Or, at least, to know of you,' the porter persisted.

'I'd better come and see her,' I said.

'By your leave, Master, I'll bring her to you. I think she could do with sitting near the fire.'

'Yes — yes, of course.'

The porter headed off to bring my mysterious guest while I refilled my tankard and engaged in the fruitless task of trying to guess who it might be. I do not have a wide circle of female admirers. In fact, since my grandmother died the circle has shrunk to a full stop.

He returned with a woman woefully ill-dressed for such weather. She wore a shawl over her normal day clothes, the only concession to the cold being her mittens. She had on a pair of dark blue woollen stockings and leather slippers which were pushed into old wooden pattens to elevate her above the cold cobbles. I turned a chair towards the fire and suggested she kick off her pattens to warm her feet.

'Can I pour you a beaker of ale?' I asked, without bothering to check there was actually a beaker to pour it into. When she nodded her thanks, I had to rummage in the room adjoining the kitchen to find one for her. I also found a plate and emptied the biscuits from the cloth onto it. She looked as if she had not eaten properly for days.

She gulped gratefully at the ale but did not touch the biscuits. 'Thank you, Master, you're very kind,' she said, then, glancing up at the concerned porter, she added, 'You both are.'

'Where have you come from on a night like this?' I asked.

'From Oegstgeest,' she said. 'I live near the Plague House.'

The Plague House was one of Leiden's white elephants. The story behind it was interesting; it was to me, anyway. In 1635 Leiden was smitten with pestilence, so the city authorities bought a parcel of land outside the city walls and built a wooden shed there to house people who had the disease. Twenty years later the plague came back, but the planned erection of a brick building had not even got as far as buying a brick. After that outbreak the city fathers were determined not to be caught out again, and built a complex of eight large halls around a courtyard, with a moat dividing the men's quarters from the women's, just in case any of the men felt like getting off their deathbeds for one last hurrah. The building was finished in 1661, since which time it had seen not a single pestilence victim. Rather than have it empty it was used periodically for anything the mayor thought of, such as a store for vegetables, an overspill for the prison, and a military hospital. It probably had other uses I know nothing about. The one thing it had never been was a plague house.

In good weather you could walk out to it in about twenty minutes, but this was not good weather. There must be some urgent reason for making the journey late at night.

'Forgive me for interrupting your evening, Master,' the woman said. 'I didn't know where to turn, then our dominie mentioned that you had solved the mystery of some young girls who went missing in Delft some years ago, and I knew I had to speak to you.'

'You're speaking to me,' I said calmly, 'and I will listen. But tell me all in good order. First, what is your name?'

'Sara,' she said. 'Sara Zwart.'

'And what's the urgency behind your visit?'

'My husband is going to be hanged for murder,' she said.

My equanimity had just fled the room. I almost dropped my tankard in surprise. 'Why?' I asked.

Sara spread her hands eloquently. 'I don't know. I can't understand it. He is not a violent man. He has never raised a hand to me, and not many wives can say that.'

I hoped that was untrue, but how would an unmarried cleric like me know? I would despise any man who struck his wife. Her home should be a sanctuary, a place of safety; to subject her to violence there is to pervert what a home should be.

She shook her head and her eyes filled with tears. 'I simply don't understand it. They just came to our house and took my husband away. And all they would tell me is that he killed someone and to say goodbye because the next time I saw him he would be dangling from a noose.'

Unsurprisingly she burst into tears again. I think I would have done so in her shoes.

'Whom is he supposed to have killed?' I asked.

'A neighbour called Wolf.'

'Where did they take him?'

'I don't know.'

There seemed no point in prolonging the conversation. I hate to see a person cry, especially myself, and my heart ached for her. Not that there was anything improper about my feelings for her. She was a married woman, and to judge by her reaction to her husband's arrest, very happily married; but she was vulnerable, and I do not believe any man is hardened enough to disregard the pleas of a young woman with tears streaking her cheeks and dropping onto her shoulders.

I urged her to eat the biscuits. Reluctantly she complied, nibbling at the first and then attacking the second with more interest.

I was looking out of the window. 'You can't go home in this.'

'I have to. I left my children with a neighbour. They'll be missing me.'

Occasionally my mouth starts to work before my brain has caught up, and this was one of those times. 'Then I'll walk with you. I'll go and fetch my cloak and boots while you finish those.'

What else could I have done?

The porter opened the door for us. 'Will you be back later, Master?'

'No, I'll find somewhere to sleep in Oegstgeest.'

'You can have my bed,' said Sara. 'I'll sleep with the children.'

'I wouldn't dream of it.'

There goes my mouth again.

CHAPTER TWO

Oegstgeest lay outside the city walls. I suppose it would not have been a good site for a plague house if it had not. Being after dark, the city gates would be shut, so we would have to persuade the gatekeeper to open it, assuming we could find him.

In those days we always seemed to be at war with someone or other, so the gatekeepers were wary of spies who might induce them to open the gate at a predetermined time of night, whereupon a troop of soldiers lurking outside would rush the gate. This meant that one person on their own was unlikely to be allowed to leave. In theory, someone could mount the walls and look for an army outside, but since anyone who did that would be a sitting duck for an archer below, it was very rarely done.

When we came to the gate, we were lucky enough to find the gatekeeper awake and sober, more or less. We explained why we wanted to leave, and he agreed to let us out, but only one at a time. He would let me go, then, if there were no consequences, Sara could follow.

'That way,' he explained, 'if you're an enemy spy, you'll know your wife's throat will be the first one slit.'

'She's not my wife,' I hastened to say.

'Well, your strumpet, then.'

'She's not that either. She's a respectable woman who wants to get home to her children. And I am Master Mercurius of the University of Leiden. Do you think I am the sort of person who would be an enemy spy?'

'I think you're exactly the sort of person they'd want,' he said. 'Who would be less likely to arouse our suspicions?'

I argue for a living. I am normally game for an argument at any time, just to keep my hand in; but there are some people you cannot argue with, and those who adopt illogical positions on the grounds that something is "the last thing you'd expect" come high on that list. 'Fine,' I said, 'just open the gate and I'll go. But how do I know you'll let Sara go?'

He looked perplexed. 'How do you mean?'

'You could just slam the door behind me and I'd be helpless while you ravaged this blameless woman.'

'Well, I wouldn't, would I?'

'But that's exactly what you'd say if you were planning to do it, isn't it?'

He scratched his head. 'I suppose so. All right, here's what we'll do. I'll open the gate, then you and I will go out, and, if it's all clear, I'll open it again from the outside to let your woman out.'

We did as he suggested, and soon we were standing outside the gate, while the hapless guard tried to work out how to open it from the outside given that there was no handle there. In the end he managed to worm the point of his knife into the gap between the doors and prise the open one forward far enough for us both to get our fingers behind it and pull it.

'Nearly a nasty moment there,' he said cheerfully as he bade us Godspeed on our journey.

There was not much moon, but the road was easy enough to see. There were isolated cottages with smallholdings surrounding them, and Sara was able to determine the fastest way to hers. We arrived around ten minutes after leaving the gate, and Sara pushed the door open to reveal a simple home. Downstairs there was a large room in which all the daily activity took place, and an alcove behind a thick curtain no doubt contained the bed used by Sara and her husband. I had always found those beds claustrophobic, especially if you were the first one in and the last one out, but I suppose if you have used one all your life it may not be so bad.

There was a ladder leading to an upper floor which extended over the parents' bed and probably included shelf beds for the children. I was glancing upwards when Sara spoke.

'My husband made them himself. He's good with his hands.'

'Then I admire him. I'm not.'

The only tool I can wield is a pen. My grandfather, my father's father, tried many times to teach me his skills at the forge, but any horse that tried to walk in shoes I had made would have looked like a sailor as he rolled from side to side. In my defence, it is much harder than my grandfather made it look.

It was my grandfather who, in a roundabout way, launched me on my career. He was a magnificent singer with a powerful voice. Our minister loved to hear him sing psalms, and it was the self-same minister who arranged for my school fees to be paid. My grandfather could not read, you see; he learned all the psalms by heart. Our minister hoped that if I could read I would help grandfather learn more songs. I am afraid that the first one I found turned out to be so obscene that my grandfather would not let me read from a songbook again. Let it be said that I had led a sheltered life and did not realise what the song was about — something to do with a maiden who welcomed a cuckoo in her nest — and my grandfather refused to tell me.

The children were in the care of a young girl of about thirteen, the daughter of a neighbour, whom Sara thanked.

'I must watch that she gets home safely, Master. We do not have the security of walls about us here.'

Sara and the girl walked back to the end of the path, and Sara stood there watching the girl's lantern as she crossed the field and walked to her own house. I was unused to the countryside at night, and what at first seemed so silent soon proved to harbour the hooting of owls, the croaking of toads and a flapping that I suppose must have been due to bats, though I admit that I saw none.

Poverty is a relative term. The family probably had little money, but they could feed themselves quite well from their smallholding, and the house was tidy and had more furniture than some. If Sara's husband had made the benches, they were well constructed and nicely finished for an amateur's effort. The children were clean and appeared well-fed, though their faces were red with crying, which they resumed when Sara returned.

'When is Papa coming home?' asked the little boy.

'I don't know, Pieter.'

'He's in jail, silly,' his big sister announced. 'You heard the men say when they came for him.'

'But he hasn't done anything wrong,' Pieter complained. 'It's not fair. Only bad men go to prison, and Papa isn't a bad man.'

Sara took the opportunity to introduce me. 'This is Master Mercurius. He's going to help us prove that Papa isn't a bad man.'

I had not actually committed myself that far, or so I thought, and rapidly replayed our conversation in my head to see if I had said anything that might be interpreted as such a promise.

The girl stepped forward. 'I'm Anneke. This is Pieter. You can call him Piet, if you like. Mummy doesn't like it, but Papa says it sometimes. Are you a minister?'

'That's right,' I said, 'but I work in the University in Leiden.'

'Are you one of those layabouts, then?' asked Pieter.

'Pieter!' said his shocked mother.

'Papa said it when he took us to the market. He said the University was full of spoilt layabouts.'

I could not help but smile. 'Your father is right about the students, but I'm a teacher.'

'What do you teach?' Anneke demanded.

'Well, mainly moral philosophy,' I said. 'Aristotelian ethical philosophy.' I could see little eyes glazing over, but I dug myself a bit deeper into my hole. 'And quite a bit about St Thomas Aquinas' commentaries on Aristotle.'

'Is that like sums?' enquired Pieter.

'It's a bit harder than sums.'

Pieter looked at me as if he now knew I was lying, because nothing is harder than sums.

'It's very late. Time you were abed,' Sara declared. 'Wash yourselves and get into bed, and I'll be up to tuck you in.'

The children washed in the basin at the end of the room, then wished me a good night and clambered up the ladder.

'It's good of you to bring me home,' Sara said. 'Please use my bed and I'll sleep on the floor.'

'Not at all,' I replied. 'You must keep the bed and I'll sleep here. I'm very used to it,' I added, not entirely truthfully.

'Are you ready to retire?' she asked.

'By all means. You must have had a long day.'

We stood looking at each other for a moment before she felt obliged to say the obvious. 'Perhaps you would turn your back, Master. I need to wash at the basin.'

'Oh! Yes. Of course. Better still, I'll go outside. You can call through the door when you're ready if I leave it slightly ajar.'

I stood outside listening to the sounds of the night and watching the twinkling stars. I had no idea why the stars seem brighter on a cold night but thought fleetingly that there would be someone at the University who knew, if I just asked the right person.

Sara called and I returned to the house. She was already sitting in her bed.

'Goodnight, Master,' she said. 'Thank you for helping us. You are a good man.'

She drew the curtain, and my thoughts at that moment were not those of a good man.

I woke once during the night, and could hear the sound of crying issuing from behind the curtain. The urge to offer comfort was great, but I could not think how it might properly be done, so I did nothing. It seemed at one and the same time the only choice and the worst choice. What use is a minister who does not offer comfort?

Morning came, and we reversed the process. I rose first, dressed and went outside while Sara got ready. Not having any experience of it, I had no idea how long it would take a woman to dress, and it was a frosty morning. I wished I had had the foresight to grab my second cloak as I left, but eventually Sara pushed open the door and invited me back in.

'You are very considerate, Master,' she smiled.

Why did God give women dimples? I am very susceptible to dimples. A happy young woman is the most glorious thing and I —

Mercurius! Remember what you are about!

She invited me to join the family at the table. There was bread and cheese, and she boiled an egg for me.

'You're not eating,' I reproved her.

21

'I'm not hungry, Master.'

'Nevertheless, you must eat. Come, have the egg.'

'I'll just have some bread,' she said, and nibbled listlessly at it.

'There is no point in your husband returning to a skeleton.'

'I would not care, if he would only return.'

After breakfast, I sat outside for a few minutes to say my prayers while Sara gave the children their chores. Despite this, Pieter immediately came to find me.

'Can you read?' he asked.

'Yes. Can you?'

'Yes. Papa taught me. I don't read big words yet, but I can spell.'

I pointed to a word on my book. 'What does that say?'

'Bible. It's a bible.'

'And do you know what a bible is, Pieter?'

'Yes, it's a book full of stories about Jesus. They kill him when he hasn't done anything wrong. Like they're going to do to Papa.'

I can only assume that Pieter had a very shallow grip on what it means to be dead, because he didn't have a lump in his throat like I did.

CHAPTER THREE

I am not a complete novice when it comes to farming, but I am seriously out of practice. The suggestion that Sara could tell me her story while I helped with the jobs that needed to be done was well-intentioned, but soon came up against the barrier of my incompetence. For a start, I am very wary of pigs, which seem to me to be untrustworthy brutes, and I have never understood why chickens rush to throw themselves under your feet when you walk into their enclosure. On top of that, my boots were not made for mud and my gown was trailing in some unpleasant substances, so Sara suggested that I should just talk to her while she busied herself. It was a distraction, she said, and the jobs must be done, although only she was there to do them.

'Who is mijnheer Zwart supposed to have killed?' I asked.

'Jaco. My husband's name is Jaco. Well, Jacobus, but we all call him Jaco.'

'Jaco, then. Who is the victim?'

Sara flicked her chin upwards in the direction of another cottage in the distance. 'A man called Wolf. Never was a man better named. He lives … lived there, in the cottage with the ramshackle fence. That was part of the problem.'

'The fence?'

'Yes. It's inadequate to keep his animals in, so they roam over other people's gardens and fields. We'd complained a number of times at finding his pig eating our vegetables, but he just laughed it off and said his pig just wanted to be in company with ours. Jaco became more and more annoyed that he wasn't taking it seriously. We can make a living here,

Master, but not much more, and we can't afford to feed other people's pigs. Do you have any idea how much a pig can eat in an hour?'

Looking at the efforts of her own pigs, I began to have some idea. 'One of yours seems to be very hungry, but the other is not eating at all.'

Sara appeared unconcerned. 'The male is a bully. He'll eat his fill, then he'll go and sleep it off and she can have whatever is left. She is content to wait, and I'll top it up if he's eaten too much. It's the way pigs are. When the piglets come, they'll be the same. There'll be a dominant one who always goes first, and the others will feed when they can.'

Very like humans, then, I thought. *There is always someone who thinks he should go first.* 'So you complained to mijnheer Wolf about his pig?'

'And his goats. Not many of us can afford to buy cows, so families keep goats instead. My friend Trijntje, the mother of the girl you saw last night, keeps a cow. She gives us milk in exchange for eggs. But Wolf had goats. It costs too much to fence all our land, Master, so we mark the boundaries with plants if we can. If goats eat them faster than they can grow, then that opens gaps for the pig to come in. You can see our problem. It can only work if everyone takes responsibility for their own animals.'

'Describe this man Wolf to me.'

'His name says it all. He was a little bit older than us, perhaps forty to forty-five. His wife died a few years ago, leaving him with their son. He's grown now, twenty or thereabouts, and every bit his father's son. Their house is a midden.'

It was said with that special contempt that Dutch women have for those who do not keep their homes clean and tidy. I had not seen the Wolfs' house, but I could imagine what my mother would have said, because I heard her say it so many times. A broom and some water make all the difference, she would tell me and anyone else who was listening, frequently said loud enough to ensure that the person being criticised could hear it too.

'He has not remarried?'

A Dutchman without a wife is like a horse without a bridle (unless he is a priest, of course). The man who loses a wife swiftly looks for another to keep the household running, and there are enough widows about to ensure that second wives can usually be found. Running a household with one adult is not easy, and the thought flitted across my mind that if Jaco was hanged Sara would soon need to find herself a new husband, after a decent period of mourning, of course.

Sara laughed. 'Who would have him? When Elisabeth was still alive, he gave her a dog's life. I walked over there once because I had not seen her for days and she would not come to the door. But I caught a glimpse of her, Master. She was one big bruise from head to foot. She had a black eye and she clutched her ribs with one arm. And he used her abominably.'

'How do you mean?' I asked.

Sara lowered her eyes. 'There are some things you should not speak of, Master.'

I did not quite grasp what she meant.

'Things between a husband and wife. Private things. Not to be done just anywhere.'

I am inexperienced in such matters, but the light finally dawned. 'Oh!'

'Yes, those things. He made demands of her anywhere, anytime that suited him. In the farmyard, in the kitchen. And it was not love, Master. We could hear her cries across the field sometimes.'

'And nobody said anything?'

'We raised it with our minister once, and he said that God had ordained the man to be the master of the household and the way in which he ran it was between a man and his God.'

'Did he, indeed? He did not quote the epistle to the Ephesians, chapter 5, for example?'

'I don't know, Master. What does it say?'

'It says "Husbands, love your wives, just as Christ loved the church and gave himself up for her", and later "husbands should love their wives as they do their own bodies", a reminder that when a man and woman marry, they become one in the sight of God.'

'Well, I have no complaint about Jaco. He is a kind husband and would never lift his hand against me.'

'Has he ever raised one against Wolf?'

Sara hesitated. 'They have had some arguments in the past. Jaco has taken the pig or goat back and they've exchanged some words. And he said that recently when they were arguing the son tried to hit him. He's a wild one, Master. A woman who married Wolf would be wary of his son. It's not healthy for a woman to be in a house with two such men.'

'What is the boy's name?'

'Joost. He came here once asking how old Anneke was. She is nearly ten, but I told him she was eight years old. I didn't like the way he looked at her, like a farmer assessing a brood cow.' She shuddered. 'The memory of that look is with me still,' she added.

'And has Wolf argued with other men?'

'Almost everyone at some time. That's why I can't understand why they have fixed on Jaco as the culprit.'

Much as I felt comfortable where I was, this was not getting Jaco Zwart released, and it was clear that Sara could not give me the information I needed. The problem was that I had no authority to investigate anything, and I could imagine that if I presented myself at the Town Hall my questions would be laughed off.

However, diligent readers of my memoirs will recall that after I unravelled a plot against his rule, William of Orange gave me a letter requiring people to assist me, in default of which they would answer to him. He had never asked me to return or destroy it, and what was it for if not to help his subjects in need? So I told Sara I had to go back to Leiden and collect some important papers before returning to Oegstgeest to speak to the mayor.

I walked back to town and had some time to think as I walked. I knew next to nothing about the crime, but plainly the first thing I had to attend to was to find where Jaco was being held and ensure that he was not hanged before I had a chance to look into the matter. Whatever Sara's beliefs were, I had to bear in mind that it was possible that Jaco was actually guilty. I know it sounds almost incredible, but once in a while the authorities arrest the right person. Quite often it is an accident, but it happens.

The law faculty at Leiden is possibly unequalled in Christendom. There are several professors there with international reputations. Those are the ones who are far too grand to speak to the likes of me. If I wanted some advice on the law, my best bet was Dr Constantijn Hop.

Hop was likely to be free because he had next to no students. Leiden had invested heavily in its Faculty of Law, bringing in some famous names from elsewhere, who had collared all the best courses. Hop spent most of his time teaching court practice to would-be advocates or hanging around the library writing increasingly recondite chapters for the book he intended to publish one day. He had explained to me once that this was concerned with wills and testaments. In the past, the property a man had to leave was real; it was land, or buildings, or piles of silver, for example. Now he might have interests to leave instead, such as a share in the United East India Company or a tenth of a fleet of ships. Suppose him to have three sons amongst whom these must be shared; who gets what? How are they to be valued? Hop was busily codifying inheritance practices into an immense textbook covering, so far as I could see, all times and all places. In fact, this was such an enormous undertaking that it was still unfinished when he died; but I get ahead of myself.

I could hear Hop's voice in the large hall. A student was seeking to convince his hearers of the merits of his client's case, and Hop interrupted loudly. 'No, no, no! You are seeking to convince learned judges sitting on the bench, not the everyday rabble in the cheap seats. Speak to them, not to the spectators.' He spotted me lurking in the corner. 'Master Mercurius! How are you?'

'Well, thank you. And you?'

'Yes, very well. Excuse us one moment while we complete this session.'

The student had another try. 'It's a civil case, mijnheer. You can't use words like "guilty".' By this point the young man was stumbling over the simplest sentence.

'Your job is to deliver the facts to the judges. Rhetorical tricks will not supplant a knowledge of the facts, mijnheer. The judges have heard it all before, and they will soon see through any attempt to replace facts with waffle. That's enough for today. Why don't you go away and just write out the facts that support your client's case? Nothing else — just those. Then tomorrow we'll try again.'

The student gathered his things and left us.

'Your pardon, Master. The things I have to do to earn a living.'

'Your student is looking for a career in the law?'

'Oh, that's guaranteed. His father is a Somebody. He'll find a position somewhere. I just pity his poor clients. The problem is that his argumentation is so poor I can't actually be sure whether he knows the law or not. Can I help you in some way?'

'If you wouldn't mind. But tell me first — are you thirsty?'

Hop grinned. 'As dry as old parchment! But I have to be back here in two hours.'

'You will be,' I promised.

We walked out into the street and debated which particular tavern to grace with our custom. Hop won, as he should, because he had visited many more of them than I had. We had struck up a friendship a couple of years earlier when we both sneaked out for an early dinner, knowing that our presence was required at a University function in the evening for which Albrecht had been doing the catering. The wise man eats first when he is going to one of Albrecht's larger dinners. No amount of free wine ever seems to hide the aftertaste of his dishes, and lately he had been seduced by a traveller's book describing how to use some of the spices from the East. I am all for experimental cookery and new experiences, but there are some things that should never be cooked with nutmeg.

When we were each sitting behind a beaker of ale, I explained what I wanted. 'I need to understand what happens when someone is suspected of a crime.'

'A particular crime?'

'A man has been murdered in Oegstgeest. His neighbour has been arrested and taken away, and his wife has asked me to prove his innocence.'

Hop nodded. 'Is she attractive?'

'What's that got to do with it?'

'I just wondered how she got you to work for nothing.'

'I'll have you know this is an act of Christian charity,' I protested.

'Good. So long as your judgement isn't being clouded by lust.'

'My judgement is rarely clouded, and never by lust.'

This was not strictly true. Actually, it was a thumping big lie. In the presence of a beautiful young woman, my judgement has frequently been overpowered. I have been known to dribble, and more than once I have hit myself in the face with a door I was opening for a woman. However, in this particular instance the woman was married, and there are boundaries I do not cross, even in my dreams.

'I'm glad to hear it,' said Hop. 'Please continue.'

'I need time to collect evidence, and I want to try to stop them judging him before I've had a chance to look into it. What will happen to him?'

Hop took a long drink and thought for a moment. 'Oegstgeest, you say?'

'That's right.'

'That's a shame. The community of Oegstgeest guards its privileges very carefully. There's little chance he'll be brought to Leiden unless they have nowhere to keep him. Does the Town Hall have a dungeon?'

'I don't know.'

'If it does, that's where he'll be. In any case they'll lock him in a room there. A municipality has the right to pronounce and carry out a sentence if the criminal has confessed.'

'He denies it, I believe.'

'I'm sure he does, but if there are adequate grounds for suspicion they can torture him a bit to get a confession.'

'When you say "torture him a bit", what are we talking about? Tickling him? Hanging him by his thumbs? Feeding him Albrecht's stamppot?'

'Good Lord, nothing as awful as that. In theory they can't do anything that will leave him permanently damaged, so nothing that involves red hot pokers or breaking bones. In practice, of course, who knows how much strain a shoulder or ankle can take before it breaks? Accidents happen, even in the best run torture chamber.'

'So if he confesses?'

'The criminal gets time to make his peace with God before his execution.'

'How long? A week?'

'No, usually a couple of hours. Sometimes overnight, if it's late in the day.'

'So if they've tortured him, he could be dead today?'

'If he confesses. If he doesn't confess, then his case is remitted to the Provincial Court. Given the caseload, that might buy him a week or two. Because Holland is such a big county, the court sits in various places, and there may not be judges free to come here for a few days. How did you plan to slow them down?'

I lowered my voice. 'I have a letter from the Stadhouder instructing public officials to render me assistance. It doesn't specify exactly what my tasks are, so I propose to tell them I'm looking into the case and that, in the name of the Stadhouder, I need them to give me some time.'

Hop took another long drink and swilled it around his mouth before speaking. 'Good luck with that. If they think the Stadhouder is trying to interfere with the independence of the courts, they'll do the exact opposite out of devilment.'

'So how do you suggest I proceed?'

'Your letter is invaluable, but they'll ask why anyone in The Hague is interested in a case in a small country town. But if it can be presented as an enquiry into the proper administration of justice in this area, and you've decided to follow one case through from beginning to end before reporting to the Stadhouder, I can pretty well guarantee you'll paralyse the machinery of justice in no time. None of these jumped up clerks will want to risk being summoned to explain their actions at The Hague.'

'Can they suffer for pursuing the case badly?'

'They can be stripped of their office, and if there's corruption they can be fined. But the biggest thing for these fellows is the stigma. In small towns, people earn prestige by their public service. They sit on the boards of orphanages and almshouses, they dole out charity or they manage the Guilds. It's expected of the well-to-do. In exchange they get their own seats in church, people bow to them in the street, and so on. Losing all that will hurt more than anything else. You could hint at that if you like.'

We drank up, I thanked him, and I went to collect my letter.

Thank goodness I could remember where I had put it.

CHAPTER FOUR

In all the years I had lived in Leiden, starting when I was about sixteen and excluding about three when I was in France and Flanders, I doubt I had visited Oegstgeest more than twice, and I have no recollection of why I had gone there even then. Now I was visiting for the second time in twenty-four hours, but this time I did not turn off towards the Plague House, but kept walking towards the woods. It was a cold day and a northerly wind was blowing, so my walk took me a good hour, but eventually I entered Oegstgeest and asked for directions to the Town Hall.

It was, of course, not as grand as its equivalent in Leiden. I introduced myself to the clerk and was delighted to see that my appearance caused something of a commotion; or, more correctly, the Stadhouder's letter did so.

In no time the back door opened and a boy sprinted out, running down the side of the building and off along the road in search of the mayor. Meanwhile, the clerk attempted to engage me in nonchalant conversation, which I frustrated by deciding upon an enigmatic silence, answering only with non-committal grunts. This was a technique that I learned from my undergraduate students who used it whenever I asked them a difficult question, so I knew just how annoying it can be.

'Would you like some hot ale, Master?'

I could hardly grunt to this question, so I accepted with thanks. It was not so much a case of wanting a warm drink, as having something hot to hold to thaw out my fingers. The clerk drew off a cup and dipped a heated iron rod in it. Unusually, his standards of hygiene were such that he did not put the rod directly into the coals, but held it in the flames for a short while. If only most taverns were as particular.

Out of the corner of my eye I could see the boy return, and after about half a minute a rotund gentleman came puffing along the side of the building and in at the back door. He must have paused a few moments to recover his breath and remove his coat, because he came through trying very hard to give the appearance that he had been working in the back room all along, an effect rather spoiled by the wetness of his boots.

'Master Mercurius! Welcome! I am Joris Gerrits, Mayor of Oegstgeest. Any emissary of the Stadhouder is welcome here. What can I do for you?'

I cannot lie. Well, actually I can, but I give myself away. Honesty is the best policy, so I tried to find a way to use only truthful sentences but convey a possibly misleading idea. 'The Stadhouder...' I began.

'Whom God preserve!' chorused the mayor and clerk.

'Thank you. The Stadhouder takes a personal interest in the administration of justice,' I said.

This much was true, if by "takes a personal interest in the administration of justice" you meant "is keen to see that certain people get hanged".

'Having been commissioned by the Stadhouder in the past to investigate certain crimes with national implications,' I continued, 'I have come to help with the investigation of a murder. I understand that a man named Wolf has been killed?'

'Yes, yes indeed,' stammered the mayor, 'but I'm afraid you may have had a wasted journey. We have the miscreant under lock and key.'

'Has he confessed?'

'Well, no, not exactly. Not yet. But he will.'

'Then we cannot conclude he is a miscreant until the Provincial Court has judged his case,' I remarked, hoping that I had remembered Hop's lesson correctly. 'Why do you conclude that this man is guilty?'

'He had been seen arguing with the victim earlier in the day, and nobody could verify his story that he was in the fields when Wolf was killed.'

'But isn't that true of most of the smallholders nearby?'

The mayor did not reply immediately. 'We haven't asked them yet.'

I decided to be conciliatory. 'Of course, you will not have had time. We must make allowances for that. In the meantime, I should like to speak to the prisoner myself. What is his name?'

'Zwart. Jacobus Zwart.'

'Is he a known troublemaker?'

'No, he has led a blameless life so far. But then that is true of all the inhabitants. This is a very law-abiding town, Master.'

'I am pleased to hear it. Has the prisoner been interrogated?'

'Not formally.'

'You mean he has not?'

'He was asked to account for himself, but no written record was made.'

'I see. Well, perhaps I can rectify that, if you have ink and paper.'

The clerk hurriedly gave me paper and an inkhorn, rushing to shape a fresh quill for me. This was done so quickly that he nicked the tip of his finger with the knife.

'This way, Master,' the mayor said, indicating a flight of stairs at the end of the building.

Zwart was being kept in an upstairs room with no window and a solid door. He had a candle, but it threw very little light. When I entered he was sitting on the floor. A filthy straw mattress was rolled at one side and he had a wooden bowl containing the remains of a meal. Since he had not eaten it all, it cannot have been that appetising. Prisoners are not normally in a position to be fussy.

'I'll bring you more light,' said the mayor. 'And a stool, of course.'

When I could see to write, I sat myself down. The mayor showed no inclination to stay, which saved me the trouble of telling him to leave.

'I am Master Mercurius, of the University of Leiden,' I explained. 'Your wife Sara has asked me to see how I can help you.'

'How is she, Master?'

'She is strong and brave, but unhappy that you cannot be home with her.'

'And the children?'

'They are well. Fortunately, they do not fully understand your position.'

'They're not alone in that, Master. I do not know how I come to be here. I've done nothing.'

'Whatever they do, you must not confess. Have they tortured you?'

'No — do you think they might?'

'Legally, they can do so to obtain a confession if they have other evidence pointing to your guilt, but they have not shown me any.'

'Executioners do the torturing, don't they? I don't think we have an executioner here. We would have to send to Leiden for one.'

It was true that we had a court at the Gravensteen in Leiden and that people were occasionally executed there. I tried not to be present on such occasions. Proponents of capital punishment tell me that it expiates the sin of the individual so that they are blameless when they stand before God, but if that were true they should execute all of us. Surely if we are blameless before God it is because Jesus Christ has paid the penalty for our sins, in which event hanging us for them seems unnecessary. What saves us is our faith, not a hanging.

'Tell me about your argument with Wolf.'

Jaco sighed. 'It seems so petty, but it's been going on for months. He won't keep his pig confined. It gets out and it causes great damage to our crops. It's not just what he eats. He digs up more than he consumes, Master. It's hard enough to feed my family as it is. I can't afford to lose a basket of turnips or cabbages every few days.'

'I can understand that.'

'I've asked him nicely. I even offered to help him repair his fence, but he refused. His goats eat the hedge, and then the pig can squeeze through.'

'Surely a pig can just push through a hedge anyway?'

Jaco gave a small laugh. 'Pigs are simple creatures, Master. They go where they can see. If they can't see through something, they try to go around it. You can round them up by walking towards them with a plank in front of you. They won't charge at you if they think you're a tree.'

I filed the information mentally, just in case I was ever faced by an aggressive pig. 'So what happened after you asked nicely?'

'The next time, I took the pig back on a rope. I told him of the damage the pig had done, but he just laughed it off as a few rotten cabbages. I wouldn't mind if he ate the rotten ones, but he digs up the best. That would have been two meals for my family. So I told him that if it happened again, I reserved the right to kill the pig. He became angry and said if I touched his pig he would do to me whatever I did to the pig.'

'You look like you could look after yourself.'

'I can fight off Wolf, but he has a son. He came at me and threatened me too. It's one or the other, but I can't fight both.'

'So you left the pig there. What happened yesterday?'

Jaco shook his head. 'I don't really know. It's all confused in my head now. Around two in the afternoon Anneke ran to where I was working and said the pig had come back. She tried to shoo it but it ignored her. I managed to force the pig out through the hedge again and steered him back to Wolf's field. We were in the lane between our two fields when a couple of women came past. They must have been the ones who said that there had been an argument. Anyway, there was a bit of pushing and shoving and some hard words, but we parted and went back to our work.

'A while later, Wolf marched over and said I had stabbed his pig. I denied it, because I hadn't, and he said to see for myself so I went with him. The pig wasn't deeply hurt, but he had a deep gash on his flank. The son was cleaning it and he dressed it with some salve. I repeated that I had not done it, but Wolf got angry. Argument was getting us nowhere, so I said I was going back to work, but Wolf followed. Then just after it was dark, the mayor's men came to the door and arrested me for the murder of Franciscus Wolf. It seems he had been found dead and his son had run to the mayor and accused me. That's all I know.'

'Sara tells me she went to see the dominie.'

'She wanted to come with me when I was brought here, but they would not let her. I don't know where she went after that.'

'She must have gone to the church, I suppose. Is this where you go to church?'

'Yes. We're Reformed. I don't know where Wolf goes, but it isn't there.'

'Your wife told me people went to see the minister when Wolf was alleged to have maltreated his wife and he declined to become involved.'

'That's true. They came to our church then, but that was in the days of the old minister. Elisabeth died just after Pieter was born, I think.'

'What took her?' I asked. 'She can't have been very old.'

'She was thirty-four. Sara might know. I think it was some women's complaint that led to a flow of blood that wouldn't stop. Then she got a fever.'

'Had Wolf fallen out with anyone else?'

Jaco chuckled again. 'Who hasn't he fallen out with? I doubt you'll find a man that Wolf or his son haven't crossed at some time. If arguing with Wolf is a reason for murder, I reckon everyone in our part of town must be a suspect.'

'It's a shame we can't make sure of the timings,' I mused.

'I tell the time by the sun, Master. That and my stomach rule my day.'

I nodded my understanding. Why would a farmer need a clock?

We knelt a few minutes in prayer and then I took my leave of him, promising to do my utmost to discover the truth and deliver him from jail.

The mayor was waiting anxiously downstairs. 'Is all in order?' he asked.

I wanted to obtain the greatest co-operation possible, so I decided to flatter him. 'First, let me praise you for your care of the prisoner. He has not been maltreated.'

The mayor seemed unduly pleased to hear this.

'I wonder, though,' I continued, 'if he might have a blanket. The room is cold.'

'I'll see to it at once,' the mayor answered. 'We may as well make his last few days comfortable.'

'It appears that Zwart was not the only neighbour who had argued with Wolf. Do you have a list of those who live nearby?'

'No. But I'm sure we can compile one.'

'Excellent. I can collect it tomorrow when I return.'

The knowledge that I planned to come back cast a shadow over his face, but at least it seemed that the mayor bore no particular animus against Jaco. He just wanted to have this matter settled, and did not mind who was convicted so long as someone was. Hanging the right man would be preferable, of course, but a speedy resolution was foremost in his mind.

'Now,' I said, 'I would like to view the body. Has a surgeon seen it?'

'No,' admitted the mayor, whose face betrayed consternation that such a thing ought to have been done. 'We have an apothecary, but no surgeon.'

'Then, by your leave, let us take mijnheer Wolf to Leiden where I can have a surgeon there examine him. You are, of course, welcome to come too, or to send a representative.'

The mayor was not a man to relish seeing a corpse opened, but neither did he want to appear to shirk his obligations. 'Alas,' he said, 'my duties here...' He spread his arms as if mere words could not express how busy he was. I could not see anything that required his attention, but perhaps the windows needed cleaning.

'Of course,' I said soothingly. 'But I would feel happier if a trusted man from Oegstgeest were present. The people here will want to know that one of their own was able to keep you fully informed.'

I do not know how small towns choose their mayors, but I was coming to the conclusion that this must have been a lean year for candidates. I think he was a good man at heart, not self-serving as some other mayors I have met have been, but inclined to pomposity (as some other mayors I have met have been). He could immediately grasp that this offered the opportunity for him to retain control of the enquiry without having to do any disagreeable work. [Marginal note: Van der Meer, you can cross out "disagreeable".]

In the absence of any other candidates the mayor nominated his clerk to go with me, and undertook to find a cart to transport the body of Wolf to Leiden.

'Where is the body?' I asked.

'In the church, Master.'

'Is it guarded?'

'No,' said the mayor. 'Who would want to steal a body?'

'I meant, from the point of view of ensuring that nobody tampers with the evidence.'

This clearly had not occurred to the mayor, but he brightened as a happy thought occurred to him. 'It was late when we transported him there, and the dominie locked it immediately after. And the body is in the vestry, which only the dominie and the verger can open.'

'Then let us hasten there and retrieve it. Unless, of course, you think that someone should stay here to guard your prisoner?'

That was something else that had obviously not occurred to the mayor. Having sent the clerk with me, he had no-one else to care for Jaco.

'I will stay here,' he declared. 'Perhaps you would allow Boudewijn to ask my daughter to come here to help me?'

It seemed that Boudewijn must be the clerk's name, because he did not wait for my approval but immediately ran out of the door and returned ten minutes later with a girl of about eighteen.

I do not know whether it is attributable to the local milk or the clean air of the countryside, but here was another woman with flawless skin. She was still pushing her hair under her cap as she entered, stopped abruptly on seeing me, and curtseyed.

'This is Master Mercurius,' said the mayor. 'He has come all the way from the University at Leiden.' He said it in awed tones as if I had rounded Cape Horn on the way, whereas a bird that flew to Leiden to Oegstgeest would probably consider it a short hop, but I let it pass.

I bowed, not a full-blown courtly bow, because there was not much room in the mayor's office and I spend too much time rubbing my backside after hitting it on objects when bowing, but a bow sufficient for the circumstances.

'This is my daughter Joanna,' announced the mayor proudly. I had the impression he was watching to see how we took to each other, in much the same way as a farmer looks at a stallion he has just introduced to his mare.

You must remember, dear reader, that I was then just past forty years of age. A quick calculation proved that I was old enough to be this girl's father. Needless to say, like most men I liked to think that I remained interesting to younger women. This feeling stayed with me until I realised that young women I was introduced to immediately started speaking slower and louder in case someone of my great age was deaf.

Nevertheless, in that moment I cannot deny that there was an attraction. She had the most wonderful hazel eyes, an unusual shade, and hair that was the colour of honey. Have you noticed that some women are incapable of a graceless movement? They sweep the floor as if they are dancing, they dip elegantly to pick something up, their hands move languidly as they speak; all this was true of Joanna.

Something in my manner must have signalled my feelings to the mayor.

'Do you have daughters of your own, Master?'

'No,' I said, then stupidly added, 'I'm not married.'

I do not know why I say that. It gets me into more trouble than anything else I say, because for some reason people take it as an invitation to match-make for me. At least there were no older women in the room, because they seem to take it as their mission in life to get me to wed their daughters, granddaughters or nieces.

I will admit that as a learned man of sober habits with a steady income — steady, but by no means munificent — I was something of a catch, but my vow of celibacy was something of a stumbling block, and I was very glad that only a few people knew that I had made it. Unfortunately, I was one of them, and I seemed unable to forget it. Believe me, I had tried on occasion. My bishop knew, of course, and by a quirk of fate at this particular time there were two such bishops because my previous bishop, Ignaas August Schetz van Grobbendonck, had just been translated to Gent, so there would be a new bishop of Namur. Pierre Vandenperre was appointed, but had not yet been installed; then, in May 1680, Van Grobbendonck unexpectedly dropped dead, and I wondered whether there was any chance that he had not got round to telling Bishop Vandenperre of my existence. As it turned out, he had. Bishop Ignaas was good with his paperwork and left everything in immaculate order.

The mayor was just getting into his paternal stride. 'When you return tomorrow, Master, perhaps you would do us the honour of supping with us?'

I know where this is leading, I thought, but I could hardly say no, could I?

CHAPTER FIVE

Boudewijn had procured a horse and cart, and together we walked along the street to remove Wolf without causing any offence.

'With respect, Master,' the verger said, 'Wolf never concerned himself about causing offence before, and I don't think he'd start now. Mind, he always said we wouldn't see him in this church again before he died, and he was right about that.'

'Why did he take against it so?'

The verger was wringing his hands anxiously. 'Well, I don't suppose it matters now if we say something about it. He and the old minister had a fearsome row.'

'What about?'

'His wife. I don't know the half of the story, probably, but it seems someone told the old minister that Wolf was beating his wife, and not just a bit of a tap now and again. The minister took it upon himself to go out to their place to see if it was true, and when he saw the sight of mevrouw Wolf he was apoplectic. He never said anything to me, mind, but Wolf himself was ranting about it in the inn later. It seems the minister told Wolf he'd better stop being so brutal to her, and Wolf said it was nobody's business but his how he treated his own wife in his own house, and if they didn't like the look of it 'twould be best if they didn't come no more.'

'Mijnheer Wolf doesn't seem to have been the best of men,' I suggested.

'It ain't done to speak ill of the dead, but I can't find a good thing to say except the Devil won't be kept waiting no longer to lay hands on his own.'

Since the verger was so voluble, I thought it might be a good idea to let him keep talking.

'What's your opinion of the man they've arrested?'

'Jaco Zwart? I knew his father. Both straight as a die. Good men, the pair of them. All I can say is that if Jaco did this, he must have been sore provoked.'

'But you think he might have done it?'

'I don't know, Master, but if not him, then who?'

'It sounds like a large number of people here had a reason to kill Wolf.'

'Yes, Master, but only one did it. The rest of us held back, but someone was pushed too far. It'll be hard to see someone swing for it, but the Lord's will be done.'

On another day we might have had a longer discussion about what exactly the Lord's will was, but time was moving on and we needed to shift Wolf. The verger found a large piece of cloth so we lifted Wolf onto the cart, packed a couple of crates each side to disguise the nature of our cargo, and covered him with the cloth. Our cart looked as if it might contain vegetables or fruit by the time we had finished.

Boudewijn took the reins, and soon the horse was heading for Leiden at a fast walk. We had a tricky moment turning over the water to get back to the city, Boudewijn not being too skilled at steering a cart which almost clipped the side of the bridge, but in around half an hour we were back at the city gate. I had forgotten that anyone taking a cart into the city was likely to be stopped, just in case any excise was due, and I held my breath as the guard made to pull back the cloth.

'May I ask you just to peek under the cloth if I untie it?' I asked.

'Why?' asked the suspicious guard.

'I don't want to cause any upset,' I explained, and untied the cloth on one side so the guard could duck his head underneath. He soon came back out again.

'We're taking him to the surgeon,' I said.

'It's a bit late for that, don't you think?' said the guard. 'I'm not a medical man, but he looks dead to me.'

'He is dead.'

'Why does he need a surgeon, then?'

I produced my letter again. 'I am Master Mercurius of the University here. I am investigating the death of this man who was killed yesterday. I need a surgeon to tell me how.'

'I should think that damn big hole under his ribs might have something to do with it,' suggested the guard. He retreated to his hut and gave me a piece of paper which he stamped. 'I assume you'll be taking him out again later,' he said. 'Just hand the paper in as you go.' He then walked away as if corpses were being wheeled in and out of the city all the time.

I had to think how best to proceed, so I told Boudewijn to take the cart around the back of the University and asked him to wait with Wolf until I found a surgeon willing to help me.

The difficulty that I anticipated was that the best surgeons were either lecturing or undertaking their extremely lucrative private practices. So far as I can see, the basis of private medicine is that someone who knows tells the patient that nothing can be done and pockets a handful of gold for saying it, but perhaps I am being unkind. I also had to bear in mind that I could not pay them for their services. All I could do was to appeal to their better natures.

That is not a strategy with much chance of success where my fellows were concerned. I mounted the steps in thought and then, as so often seems to be the case, Providence extended a helping hand, because at the top of the steps I encountered the Rector.

Dr Drelincourt was a physician, but before coming to Leiden he had been an inspector of army hospitals, so it was likely that he knew something about surgery, and, by the look of things, he had nothing pressing to do at that moment.

'Good day, Master Mercurius,' he said.

As a result of my studies in France and Flanders, I could speak something approaching French, and since I wanted something from him I replied in that language. 'Good day, Rector. A beautiful day, if a little cold.'

'Indeed it is, Master.'

'Rector, may I ask you something?'

'Of course.'

This required some finessing. How could I explain that nobody had actually asked me to do what I was doing and still ask for help? 'You may not yet be aware, Rector, that a woman came to the University for help last evening.'

'No, I was not,' said Drelincourt, his eyes betraying his concern.

'I happened to be available to speak to her. It appears that her husband had been arrested for murder and she hoped someone might be able to prove him innocent.'

'I see,' said the Rector.

'I have visited Oegstgeest, where the crime was committed, but they have no surgeon there who can tell me how the deceased met his end. I was hoping you might be willing to examine him.'

'I should be glad to do so, Mercurius, but I have an appointment here in a couple of hours. That would not give me time to go to Oegstgeest to view him.'

'No need, Rector! I have brought the body here. It is in the rear court.'

Drelincourt looked at me as if I had desecrated the relics of several of his favourite saints. 'You have brought him here?'

'You must agree, Rector, that there is no institution better placed to conduct a thorough and Christian examination than this university?'

'Well, that goes without saying, but I hope there has been no offence caused to any on the way?'

'The corpse is decently covered.'

The Rector was caught, having said that he would willingly examine Wolf before he realised he was just a few paces away, so he sighed and began rolling back his sleeves. 'Lead the way, Mercurius.'

At the Rector's direction, Boudewijn and I carried Wolf into one of the rooms alongside the court and laid him on a table. The Rector walked slowly round the body, occasionally crouching to observe something more closely and sniffing once or twice. He began gently probing the torso with the flat of his hand. 'He works hard for his living. Observe the development of the musculature. Yet, I think, not so hard now as once he did. There is a lot of fat in his upper arms. The liver is enlarged, and he has the smell of a drinker.'

In these more fastidious days the import of this comment may be missed, so let me explain that to get a reputation as a drinker in Leiden back then you had to spend a good proportion of your time laid horizontally.

Drelincourt left the room briefly to fetch his instruments, selected the tool most suited to his needs, and plunged it into Wolf's breast near the top, dragging it down to a little below his navel. He then peeled back the skin. There will be no further description of the procedure because I was engrossed in examining the ceiling, the windows, and anything else I could find that did not require me to look at the table.

'That's interesting,' said Drelincourt a couple of times, but without enlightening me as to what had attracted his attention. At length he replaced the skin and closed it with some stitches, treating Wolf as carefully as he would have done a live patient. 'Let us make him look his best for his burial, shall we?'

Drelincourt poured water into a bowl and washed Wolf's face, combing his hair and folding his arms across his chest, this last being rendered more difficult by the rigor mortis which had invaded his muscles and was not dissipating due, Drelincourt explained, to the cold. With some massaging and manipulation Drelincourt managed to arrange the body in a suitable position, covered him once more with the cloth, and then washed his hands before rolling his sleeves down and addressing us.

'The cause of his death is a single fierce blow with a knife, entering the body just below the ribs on the left side but angled upwards. It has penetrated the large lower chamber of the heart and caused a great loss of blood. Death would have been very quick. The normal heart pumps about a gallon of blood each minute, and a considerable fraction of this was leaking into the cavity around the heart. Nevertheless, you will see from the webbing between his fingers and thumbs that he used both hands to try to pull the knife out. He has cut himself on the edges of the blade, so clearly some of the blade protruded from the body, and yet the wound is very deep. I think,

Mercurius, that the weapon used had a blade at least a foot in length.'

'Not a standard knife such as a man might carry for his work, then?'

'He might have it in a tool-bag, Mercurius, but not about his person, I should think. And there's something else. Look at the wound, and you see a sharp edge on one side, but not the other. This is a cut made by a single-sided knife.'

'Zwart was not arrested until some hours later, but no mention was made of a knife, nor do I think any attempt was made to find one.' I looked to Boudewijn for confirmation of this oversight, but it was now his turn to admire the ceiling.

'Then you must discover whether he ever had such a knife or, if not, who did. His liver is enlarged, so I suspect that he spent his evenings in a tavern. His life would have been shortened anyway by his own dissipated mode of life.'

'Thank you, Rector. Is there anything else you wish to draw to my attention?'

'Yes,' the Rector replied, 'look at his left foot.'

I did so but I could see nothing of interest to our investigation. 'What am I looking at, Rector?'

'He has six toes. You don't see that very often.'

The Rector was nothing if not thorough. By the time we had returned Wolf to the cart and tied him securely in place, he had reappeared from his office with a signed report in his own hand. Unusually for a senior academic, his handwriting was entirely legible.

I thanked him, and we began the journey back to the church. The paper that the guard had given us in the morning proved successful in getting us allowed out without awkward explanations, and by late afternoon we were rolling sedately into Oegstgeest once again. The locals eyed us quizzically as if bemused by any cargo a minister and their town clerk could possibly have secured for them, but apart from a few tipped hats there was no interaction with them, and soon Wolf was back in the vestry.

The verger gazed steadily at the corpse. 'I don't know as I ever saw him clean before. I've a mind to give him a shave if there's no objection, Master?'

'No, none,' I said.

'I like to ensure that they're looking their best when they meet their Maker. I hope someone will perform the same office for me when the time comes, but I pray God that won't be soon, for I've a deal of work to do here before the spring arrives.'

I left Wolf in the care of the verger and sought out the mayor.

'Master! Welcome back. Was your journey successful?'

'It was, Mayor, thank you. The Rector himself conducted an examination of the body and has given me his report.' I handed it to the mayor, who unfolded the sheet with all reverence.

'The Rector himself? We are honoured. See, here is his seal!'

I could foresee the page being framed and hung on a wall somewhere for the citizens to gawp at. Many of them would have no idea what it said, but they would probably recognise that a missive with a red wax seal is important. 'Did you discover a knife as described there amongst mijnheer Zwart's possessions?'

'No, it was not about him. We must go to his home and search there.'

'By your leave, Mayor, it grows dark, and I doubt that his wife will hide such a knife because she would not know that we were looking for it. It can wait until morning. Perhaps I can accompany the constables?'

'We would be honoured. But you are right about the time. Why not bring my invitation forward, Master, and sup with us now? And you are welcome to stay the night. We have a spare bed.'

'I would not wish to impose,' I began uncertainly, because actually imposing in this way seemed very desirable. The wind was beginning to howl, squalls of sleet were blowing confusedly around in the street, and a convivial evening with the lovely Joanna was an extremely enticing prospect.

'Nonsense!' cried the mayor. 'No imposition at all. The company will be very welcome.'

And in no time we were striding into the hail in the direction of a large house through the windows of which I could see the welcoming glow of a good fire.

CHAPTER SIX

If my sudden appearance in their home caused any consternation to mevrouw Gerrits and her daughter, they hid it well. I was shown into the parlour and a goblet of good wine was thrust into my hand, then I was invited to sit near the fire and converse with mevrouw Gerrits while the mayor gave new instructions to the cook and juffrouw Gerrits disappeared to her chamber to make herself more presentable for company. In the fleeting glimpse I caught of her as we arrived there seemed little room for improvement in her appearance, but she excused herself and ran upstairs as if I had caught her bathing in the kitchen.

I suppose that if your husband is a mayor you will be adept at small talk, particularly with people you know nothing about, and mevrouw Gerrits was soon probing me gently for information. She was very easy to talk to and in no time she had discovered my job, my employer and my marital status and was now moving on to discuss the reason for my visit to Oegstgeest.

'It is, I'm afraid, not a happy one. I have worked in the past for the Stadhouder —'

'Whom God preserve,' she quickly inserted.

'Indeed, whom God preserve. His Excellency likes to reassure himself that the citizens of the United Provinces are receiving justice properly administered. Having heard that we had a murder right on our doorstep, so to speak, it seemed a good opportunity to observe how things were done here and to offer whatever small assistance I might be able to render.'

'My husband will be glad of it, I'm sure, Master. This is a new experience for him.'

I did not like to tell her that it was hardly a regular experience for me either. Despite repeated contact with undergraduates, we have not had a murderer amongst our teaching staff (so far as I know).

The door opened and juffrouw Gerrits entered. Joanna was now clad in a dark blue dress, stiff-bodiced, and with something of a train behind. It dropped off her shoulders and yet by some witchery it fell no further. I realise that my descriptions of women's clothing could be better, but it is not a subject in which I have had much instruction.

She dipped in welcome and sat on a long padded bench against the wall.

'Come nearer the fire, my dear,' her mother instructed, which meant that Joanna had to take the remaining available chair, next to my own. I rose again until she was seated. 'I hope your expectations are not too high, Master,' mevrouw Gerrits continued. 'We do not often have the opportunity to entertain.'

'I am very grateful that you are prepared to tolerate the disorder I must bring to your household,' I answered.

'Not at all. The meal will be about ten minutes, I believe. Joanna, will you not play a little music to entertain Master Mercurius?'

'Oh, Mother, Master Mercurius will be accustomed to much better playing than I can manage,' protested Joanna.

'Nonsense,' said her mother firmly. 'I would not ask if I did not know that you play well.'

Joanna rose and walked to the corner of the room. From a small chest there she drew a flute and a recorder, hesitated a moment, then put the flute down and commenced to play the recorder.

I am not musical, but I had no idea that it was possible to mimic birdsong so accurately on any instrument. I could distinctly hear a nightingale singing. Once she had begun to play, Joanna was wrapped up in her music and was soon swaying gently as she played.

I imagine that audiences at recitals are expected to watch the players' hands, but I was increasingly drawn to those undulating hips. I have no idea how long she played, but it was not nearly long enough. I would have sat happily all evening and most of the night watching her play.

The spell was broken when I noticed her mother inspecting me for my reaction, which prompted me to move my eyes a little higher, close my mouth and discreetly check whether I had been drooling. Unfortunately, raising my eyes did not work either, because on the way from her hips to her mouth my gaze caught other objects of some interest, particularly when she breathed deeply before a long phrase.

At the end I broke into fevered applause, not minding for a moment that I was alone in doing so. 'That was remarkable!' I exclaimed.

'You are too kind, Master,' said Joanna. 'Would you care to play something?'

'I don't play, I'm afraid. But I greatly admire those who do,' I added quickly.

'There you are, Joanna,' her mother said. 'Just think how well you would play if you would only practise now and again.'

'I do practise, Mother,' the girl protested. 'Not, perhaps, every day, but regularly.'

The mayor entered. 'What's this? Have you been playing for our guest?'

'Indeed she has, Mayor, and enchantingly too.'

'She is a very accomplished young lady,' the mayor told me. 'When the time comes, she will make a fine wife for some lucky man.'

I felt that some comment was expected, so I provided one. 'Undoubtedly.'

'Father, you're embarrassing our guest,' Joanna muttered.

'No, I'm not. He is a man of good sense and knows that all that matters is whether my statement is true or not, and he can form his own opinion on that.'

'Then you're embarrassing me!' she hissed, blushing prettily.

If this were a romance I would have jumped up at once, seized her hand and declaimed, "Come, let us elope and seek our fortunes together in Amsterdam!" but as this was real life I just thought it instead, then passed a few minutes mentally enumerating the reasons why such a notion was impractical.

First, I had no idea how she would take such an invitation. I like to think that I possess some virtues of solidity, dependability, and sober life, all of which must be attractive to a certain type of woman. Well, my grandmother regularly listed them as my chief virtues anyway.

Second, I would not want to have to explain to the Rector that I was abandoning the University in mid-year with no notice. He was a tolerant and enlightened man, but such an announcement would test both of those qualities.

Third, I did not actually want to go to Amsterdam. Given what the Lord did to Sodom and Gomorrah in response to the sin there, I am constantly astonished that Amsterdam is not sitting in a lake of sulphurous fire. There are things that go on in the docks there that I could never set down in a book, even if I had the ability to describe them.

The food was brought, and I was shown to a seat. When we were all accommodated, the mayor invited me to say Grace, which I did, and we began to eat.

If this was their ordinary fare, then the mayor and his family ate very well indeed. I had half a mind to ask for the recipes so that I could give them to Albrecht, but it would have been in vain. Albrecht has many recipes, and his food often looks very appetising — until he comes to cook it. There are times when I want to fling open his oven door to see if Shadrach, Meshach and Abednego are walking around in there.

Obviously we could not discuss the murder in front of the ladies, so we were restricted to the ordinary conversation of the table; if, that is, the ordinary conversation at table can be said to include thinly veiled inducements to persuade me to settle in Oegstgeest and marry their daughter. I was reminded that it was just a brisk walk to the University, that houses were cheaper there than in the city, which is not surprising given where the Plague House was, and even that the minister had not settled in well since his arrival and was beginning to wish that he had stayed in Rotterdam.

We resumed the chairs by the fire, and Joanna was directed to read to us by her father. Whether it was in deference to my cloth or evidence of a pious household, she chose to read from the Bible, settling on a portion of the book of Job, exactly the sort of reading suited to a typical Dutch Calvinist family but somewhat of an odd fit with a delightful meal. She read well and had a pleasant voice, not too high-pitched like some girls'.

All too soon it was time to retire, and I was shown to my room. After a brief tour of the house to show me the necessary offices, I was ready for bed, and said goodnight to my hosts. Joris and his wife crossed the landing, while Joanna slipped into her bedroom.

Right next door to mine.

[Marginal Note: Van der Meer showed undue excitement here. 'You can't finish dictating there!' he said. 'What happened next?' What happened next is that I went to sleep and woke up in the morning. Not without some diverting fantasies in my dreams, I will admit.]

We breakfasted early and left the house just as the ladies were coming downstairs. I had almost forgotten the purpose of my visit and had to recap the information we had in my mind to ensure that I made the most of my time.

I took my leave of the mayor and walked to Wolf's gate. I pushed it open, watching warily for the pig, and looked around for his son. Joost was at the back of the house, scattering feed for the chickens.

'Who are you?' he demanded.

'I am Master Mercurius of the University of Leiden,' I replied, 'here to help the mayor to investigate the unfortunate death of your father. I offer you my prayers and sympathy.'

'Thank you,' he answered, 'but what is there to investigate? The man who killed him is in custody and will shortly hang.'

'Only if the judges believe that there is evidence that he killed your father. My job is to collect all the evidence.'

Joost shook his head violently. 'He did it! That's all they need to know.'

'Perhaps. But they don't know that. We have to produce evidence to prove the point. Let's begin by hearing your account of what you saw, if you don't mind.'

Joost shook his head again at this waste of time, but finally began. 'I was round here mucking out the animals. Or I may have been carrying the dung to the fields. Either way, I wasn't there to see exactly what happened.'

'I see. When was this?'

Joost thought for a few moments. 'Probably around three o'clock. Zwart brought the pig back and he and father had a row. Then a bit later we noticed that the pig had a gash in his side.'

'Not one that could be made by a thorn or bramble, for example?'

'No, far deeper than that. Zwart must have taken a knife to it. We hadn't noticed when the pig came back because he was dirty, but now we could see the blood running down his flank. Father went to sort it with Zwart.'

'You didn't go?'

'Father told me not to. He said it should be one man to one man. Anyway, Zwart came back with him to see the pig. I was dressing the wound by then. There was some more arguing and a couple of women heard them at it. Zwart stormed off and we returned to our labours. Then I heard Father say something, not a proper word, just a noise, so I came to tell him I hadn't heard and to ask what he wanted, and he was lying on his back on the ground, just a couple of paces from the gate.'

'Was he still alive?'

'Barely. He was in a sort of swoon. And within a very short time he was dead.'

'Was the knife anywhere about?'

'The knife?' Joost looked around. 'I didn't notice. I didn't see one. It wasn't still in him, if that's what you're asking.'

'So what did you do?'

'I don't know exactly. I tried slapping his face gently, then a bit harder, but he didn't recover. Then I thought I should go for help, but there was no point in asking for help from the man who'd just killed him, so I ran up the road.'

'To summon some help?'

'That's right. Some men came to look after Father.'

'Was your father still where you had left him?'

'Of course he was. You don't think he was going to stand up and walk about a bit, do you?'

'No, but you had left him unattended. Quite understandably, of course, but I just wanted to be sure that when the men arrived they would have seen just what you saw.'

'Exactly the same. Then they told me I must take him to the mayor. I thought he would know what to do. I told him the story just as I have told you, and he summoned some men and came back with me.'

'When did the mayor get here?'

Joost was becoming exasperated by my questioning. 'How should I know?'

'Well, was it dark?'

'It must have been. I remember it was just turned dark by the time someone had made our cart ready and we had loaded Father into it, then walked it to the church. I had to find a lantern to guide our way.'

'Thank you, mijnheer Wolf. You've been very helpful.'

Joost nodded curtly.

'What will you do now?' I asked.

'Me?'

'Are you going to carry on with the farm?'

Joost stood with his hands on his hips and looked about him. 'This is all I know, but there's barely a living for one man here, let alone two. We need a cow or two, perhaps another pig, but I've no way of getting one. Unless, I suppose, people take pity on us and give us alms. I hear in some places there's a collection in honour of the man who has died.'

I made a mental note to see if there was some method of seeking charity for Joost to give him a good start in his new life, thanked him again, and walked out into the lane.

Rather than go directly to the Zwarts' house, I walked down the lane a little way until I was sure that Joost was not watching, then I doubled back and knocked on the door of the cottage. There was no reply, but I heard Pieter calling somewhere outside, so, assuming that his mother would be near, I walked towards the cries.

Pieter was ignoring his mother's repeated commands to keep himself clean. She lost her patience with him and pulled him roughly off the ground. I think she was about to smack him when she saw me approach, and instead she used her raised hand to brush him down.

'Now, run and play while I talk to the Master,' she said. She looked at me guiltily. 'I'm sorry,' she said. 'It's all been a bit much for me. I worry about Jaco and I can't manage two high-spirited children such as mine. If I'd hit him, I'd have felt bad afterwards. He's only a child. He doesn't understand that he's vexing me.'

Her eyes began to run with tears and she turned away so that I should not see. I offered her my handkerchief, which she used to dab her eyes.

'Thank you, Master,' she whispered, 'you're very kind.'

Once again I felt constrained not to offer the comfort that I might have done, and wanted to give. Those tears had glazed over the deep blue eyes and the cheeks were reddened by crying. Being smaller than I was, she tipped back her head endearingly to look up at me. Her lips were slightly parted, my attention drawn to them because the lower one was trembling. I wanted to wrap my arms around her and tell her that all would be well in the end, but I could not. Her husband was still the main suspect — indeed, the only suspect — in the murder of her neighbour. Unless I came up with something better than my mere feeling that he was innocent, then he would hang, and I could not tell her otherwise.

CHAPTER SEVEN

Looking back on the events of that day, I can see that my actions did not conform strictly to those which the proper application of logic required. My purpose in being there was to look for a murder weapon, but as one man searching a relatively large smallholding my chances of finding it would be almost nil, so I opted to check whether such a weapon had ever been there.

'Does Jaco possess a knife?' I asked. I suppose if Sara had said no, my enquiry would have come to a complete and premature stop.

'Yes,' she said, 'several. Why do you want to know?'

'I need to inspect them to see if any of them could be the murder weapon.'

Sara looked shocked. 'You don't think he did it? Not you too.'

'It's not a question of what I think. It's simply that if he doesn't possess the murder weapon, then I'm justified in looking for someone else who might.'

Sara was confused. 'So do you think he did it or don't you?'

'That isn't how it works. They need evidence to convict him. Without that, he'll be acquitted. But unless someone else is prosecuted, there would always be a cloud over Jaco's reputation.'

She nodded. 'Nowhere more so than here. Gossip thrives, and nobody cares too much about facts before they open their mouths.'

'Well then — where does he keep his knives?'

Sara took me into the house and pointed at a small chest by the door. 'They'll be in there. We can't leave them where Pieter might get his hands on them, the little devil, or he'll harm someone with them. He'd only be playing, but he doesn't understand about knives.'

The chest had holes bored in the top and front through which a thin rope was looped and knotted to make it secure. Given enough time even Pieter might get into it, but presumably the plan was that he would never be left alone with the chest for long enough.

I squatted and began to unpick the complex knot that kept it closed. After a couple of minutes, I was sorely tempted to let Pieter have a try because he might do better than I was, but I persevered and eventually the lid was released.

There were two immediate observations.

'Sara, this knot doesn't look like it has been released recently. Does Jaco have none anywhere else?'

'There was a knife he used every day that he kept on his belt. It would have been with him when he was arrested.'

'They would have taken that off him for their own protection. He didn't leave it here?'

Sara looked around distractedly. 'I don't know. It was all so sudden and I was tearful. I didn't notice.'

Pieter ambled across from his play. 'What are you looking for?' he asked me.

I knelt down so I could look him in the eye and appear less threatening to a small child. 'When the men came for your papa, did you see where they put his knife?'

Pieter cogitated as he chewed on a biscuit. 'Oh, that,' he said. 'It's in the cupboard by the basin.'

'When did they put it there?' asked Sara. 'They never came up this end of the room.'

'No, I put it there,' Pieter explained. 'You can't leave knives lying around, you know. It's dangeristic.'

Sara opened the cupboard and then stood back as if I should be the only person to touch the knife. I lifted it out of the dark recess and laid it carefully on the table.

'He's cleaned it,' I said.

'Of course he's cleaned it,' Sara answered. 'He's very particular about his tools. You can't put them away dirty or they'll spoil.'

The knife I was looking at was stout, with a wooden handle about twice the thickness of my little finger and a blade of about the same thickness at the top, tapering to a point; but the blade was no longer than my hand. Driven in hard, it could have pierced Wolf's heart and then been withdrawn enough to allow Wolf to grasp the top of the blade with his hands, but Drelincourt had not seen any imprint or bruise caused by the handle striking the skin, nor was there any blood on the handle of the knife. Given that the wooden handle was unvarnished, it would have been quite hard to remove every trace of blood had there been any. I was convinced that I was not looking at the murder weapon. Apart from other considerations, if the blade had been driven in so far, the opening in Wolf's body would have had to be wider to accommodate the blade.

I took the other knives from the chest. It seemed unlikely that they had been moved in recent days, because there was a thin layer of dust, but even if they had, none of these seemed exactly right. The most likely one was a blade which was elongated and narrow.

'What is this used for?' I asked.

'It's a boning knife, Master. It's used in butchery. When we kill the pig, it can be used to separate the meat from the bone.'

'And this is the only one you have?'

'Yes, Master. We only use it on the pig.'

I shook my head. 'It's too short to have inflicted the wound on Wolf.'

The absence of a murder weapon was not conclusive, of course. Jaco could have disposed of it immediately after the killing; and it was by no means certain that his wife would have known all the knives that he had. However, they seemed to be a couple who knew each other's business very well, and they lived in such a small cottage that there were few places where anything could be concealed.

I thanked Sara and made to leave, but she clutched my arm.

'Pray for us, Master! Please say you'll pray for Jaco to be released soon and returned to us.'

'With all my heart.' I meant it. I was attracted to Sara, but she was another man's wife, and I am not such a villain as to take advantage of the situation to tempt her astray. Wherever "astray" is, which I am not too sure about.

'Master, why does God allow these bad things to happen to us? We are not great sinners, that such a horror should be visited upon us.'

If this had been the classroom, I might have suggested that Sara direct her question to my professor, Professor Spanheim, who could easily have spoken extemporaneously on the subject all afternoon. Theodicy, the justification of God in the face of the evil in the world, is not my speciality. This is partly because I have better things to do with my time, but mainly because it is one of the areas of theology where the Catholic and Reformed teachings differ and I have not really made up my mind which is to be preferred.

Following St Augustine and St Thomas Aquinas, we Catholics believe that God can have no responsibility for evil because, being goodness itself, He has no capacity for it. Evil arises because men and women have free will and, being corrupted by original sin, use their freedom wrongly. As a Reformed minister, however, I grew up believing that evil is due to some of us being predestined to be damned and that therefore God has no interest in reforming these people because He does not want them in Heaven anyway. On balance, I think I prefer a solution that says some of us are bad some of the time to one that says some of us can do nothing other than being bad, but this was not the place to debate it.

'Sometimes God allows us to be tested, Sara. He does not promise us a soft or easy life, and we all ride the waves of fortune. We show our devotion to Him in the way that we deal with these events. But He is never unjust. If Jaco is innocent, he will not be allowed to suffer indefinitely.'

'What do you mean, "If Jaco is innocent"? I thought you believed me.'

'I do. I meant since, not if.'

Sara turned away from me and covered her face with her apron. 'I could not bear to lose him,' she sobbed. 'What would be the point of life without him?'

This sounded horribly as if she intended to lay violent hands upon herself. The church teaches that this is a grave sin, with terrible consequences for the soul. Those of us of a more compassionate bent try to prove that such people are out of their senses when they do these things.

'Have faith,' I said. 'It will not come to that.'

'Do you promise me?' Sara said.

'Yes,' I answered, as firmly as I could.

I have no idea why I make these promises that I cannot keep, but I do.

She wrapped me in her arms and kissed me on the side of the neck. This was not undue passion; she could not reach any higher. Even so, it was not a normal component of relations between ministers and the laity, and I felt more than a little awkward.

'I must go now,' I said. 'Perhaps you will allow me to take the boning knife so I can prove to the mayor that it cannot be the murder weapon.'

'Gladly, if it helps Jaco,' Sara said.

I closed the gate behind me and took a deep breath. That interview had not gone the way I had expected. I began to wonder if I was allowing my sympathy for Sara to overpower my judgement where Jaco was concerned.

When I reached the town hall in Oegstgeest, Boudewijn leaped to his feet. 'Master, I have something for you,' he exclaimed, and unrolled a sheet of paper tied with a blue ribbon. It was a crudely drawn sketch showing the town. 'Forgive the lack of detail, Master. I did it in haste.' He pointed at the large building at the top of the sheet. 'That is where we are now. Here you see the road to the mayor's house, leading to the east. The road towards the Plague House is here, leading south, then bending to the south-west. I have marked Wolf's cottage with the letter W, and Zwart's is across the lane, marked with a Z.'

So much was clear, but in truth I had walked that lane often enough in the past three days to be able to draw this myself. The value in Boudewijn's work lay in the other eight marks on the map.

'There are eight other homesteads on that side of the town, Master. Heading northwards from Zwart's house on the left side of the road you come first to Abraham Venstra. He lives there with his wife and, I think, four children. Next is Wim Pienaar. He is Venstra's wife's uncle, an older man. His wife is still alive but their children are all grown. One lives on the other side of town near the mayor. I don't know about the rest. The last cottage on that side belongs to Claas van 't Bos. His father died a year or so ago. Claas recently married, a nice girl, not from this town. They met at the market in Leiden. On the other side of the road, leading up from Wolf's farm, we have the widow De Boer. She lives alone, but she employs some boys from the town to do work for her. She is one of the women who were walking past when they heard the argument between Zwart and Wolf.'

'Who was the other?'

'Ah, her neighbour, mevrouw Hoeks. Her husband Lenaert is one of the elders of our church. You can trust her testimony completely. The family are all ardent Calvinists.'

That was not exactly a recommendation in my eyes, but I could hardly say so, since I was doing my best to appear to be one myself. It was uncharitable of me, since they were probably doing their very best to live blameless lives, as I was myself. I just hoped they were not of that variety of Calvinism that disapproves of any kind of fun.

'Then the next farm belongs to Jan and Griet Smulders.' Boudewijn lowered his voice confidentially. 'Jan is a good man, but he is too fond of tavern company.'

Next he pointed at a house set behind the Smulders' farm and accessible only by a narrow track.

'That is the home of Piet Aelter. Now, I draw your attention particularly to this one because he and Wolf have had words before. If you will kindly look here, you will see that I have drawn a line at the south side of Aelter's farm. He shares that boundary with Wolf's smallholding, and they have had several arguments about that boundary and where exactly it runs. It all came to a head last summer when Aelter came here accusing Wolf of having moved the boundary markers. Wolf said he had done no such thing, and when the boundary was inspected and it was shown that at least two of the markers had moved from their original positions, he suggested they must have shifted in the heavy rain. Well, perhaps, but they had never moved before.'

I looked at the map with puzzlement. 'Isn't Aelter's farm uphill from Wolf's?' I said.

Boudewijn smiled. 'Yes, Master. The markers must have floated uphill on the floods and been stranded there.'

'Are they wooden?'

'No, Master. Old millstones. They don't float well.'

It was clear that mijnheer Wolf was no innocent. I was sure that I would soon find other examples of arguments and slights. 'Mijnheer Wolf seems to have had a special gift for causing controversy.'

'There is more, Master. But permit me to finish the map first. Round the bend in the road you come to Matthaeus and Hanna Pijl.' Boudewijn lowered his voice once more. 'They are notorious Catholics.'

'In what sense, notorious?'

'Well, they do not attempt to hide the fact, Master. They walk to Leiden every Sunday to attend Mass somewhere.'

I know what you are thinking, dear reader. I must have met them at some time at Mass; but remember that I was under instructions to keep my faith secret, so I only attended Mass outside Leiden. Most Sundays you would find me in the Pieterskerk, masquerading as a good Protestant. If you were particularly fortunate, you might even see me in the pulpit about twice a year in one or other of Leiden's Reformed churches.

'Why have you picked out these eight, Boudewijn?'

'First, Master, because they are nearest, but also because at the time of the killing there was a meeting here in town. So far as I can tell, most of the men of the town were there. And I assume that it is out of the question that a woman could have done this terrible act.'

'Not quite, Boudewijn. I have heard of women stabbing men, but I grant it is uncommon.'

'The other reason for thinking it must be one of these men is mevrouw Hoeks.'

I was intrigued. 'Explain yourself, Boudewijn.'

The expression on his face was ample proof that he had hoped not to have to explain his line of thought. He had hoped that it spoke for itself, but it was barely whispering to me. 'I hate to speak ill of such upstanding people…'

'But?'

'Well, nothing much happens in the lane that mevrouw Hoeks does not see. It is unlikely that anyone passed that way without her noticing. She even had the house rearranged so she can work at the front window.'

'And she saw nothing?'

'She hasn't said anything about it if she did, but I suppose it is something we will have to check.'

I did not miss the use of the first-person plural pronoun. Still, it would be good to have some assistance, because frankly I was not sure where to go next in this enquiry.

CHAPTER EIGHT

'Let's talk to the two women who heard the conversation first,' I suggested.

Boudewijn was delighted to have a pretext for leaving the town hall, and rushed to collect his cloak. Since the mayor was not around, he wrote a sign explaining that he had been called away on urgent business and tacked it to the door.

'Who is our first call?' he asked.

'I think the widow De Boer. But if she and mevrouw Hoeks are speaking together, we will go somewhere else first. I do not want them to agree on a story, particularly if, as I think you were hinting, mevrouw Hoeks is a dominant woman.'

'Dominant — that's the very word, Master.'

For a moment I thought Boudewijn was looking for paper to write it down so he could use it again later, but he was just checking that I had not left his map.

'This way, Master!'

I knew the way, of course. I had walked past the house twice in the last hour or so, though I paid it no attention. 'You said she employs men from here to do her work.'

'Boys, really, Master. No more than fifteen or sixteen, but strong and willing. There's never any shortage of boys wanting to work there, because she pays well.'

'How is she able to afford that?'

'She may be an unfortunate widow, Master, but you try to get even one duit off the price of anything you're buying from her.'

I have never been a good haggler, and while I might haggle over a stuiver or two, I wouldn't bother about a duit; but then

I have plenty. The parable of the widow's mite came to mind. Given that there are a hundred and sixty duits in a guilder, Boudewijn was painting a definite picture of the woman we were about to meet, to whom even a duit was important.

We arrived at the cottage. It was immaculate, freshly whitewashed, with a sound door. I had been expecting a little frail old lady, but it was soon clear that the wages might not have been the only attraction here. Mevrouw De Boer was a sturdy, well-presented woman in her middle years.

I introduced myself and Boudewijn.

'Ah, yes,' she said, inspecting him critically. 'The mayor's underling.'

'He is helping me with the investigation of the death of mijnheer Wolf,' I explained. Mevrouw De Boer looked at me as if to say that my inquiry was doomed to failure from the outset, given my choice of assistant. *There must be a story behind that*, I thought, and resolved to ask it as soon as may be. 'I understand, mevrouw, that you were a witness to an altercation between mijnheer Wolf and mijnheer Zwart shortly before the death.'

'I was, as was mevrouw Hoeks. We had been to Leiden to buy good flour.'

'Doesn't anyone here grind flour?'

'Yes, but there is only one, therefore the price is higher. In Leiden one has more choice, and therefore millers are more likely to strike a bargain. We buy a sack between us, you see, which means it stays fresher.'

'But surely it is a long way to carry a sack?'

'We don't bring it back with us. It is delivered by a carrier along with the rest of our purchases.'

I had the feeling that I had been added to her mental list of men who are too stupid to know that a lady cannot carry a sack. 'Perhaps, mevrouw, you would describe the argument you overheard to us.'

'We walked up the lane together. Mevrouw Hoeks has the next house, you see. As we came round the corner we were talking, and then the most remarkable thing happened. Mijnheer Zwart must have been to the Wolf house and he walked out into the lane, then shortly afterwards mijnheer Wolf chased after him using the filthiest language.'

'Did you understand what mijnheer Wolf was so upset about?'

'Not entirely. His pig came into it somewhere. I shouldn't be surprised if it hadn't broken out and gone roaming again. I've had to shoo him away myself from time to time.'

'In your opinion, was mijnheer Zwart angry or in a hurry to fetch a weapon?'

'He wasn't running, if that's what you mean. He was clearly annoyed, but the ferocity of Wolf's attack came as a surprise to him, I think. I had the impression they had already had an argument and Zwart thought it was over, then it started up again.'

'When did you become aware that Wolf had been stabbed?'

'I was in my kitchen when I heard Joost shouting.'

'Thank you. You clearly know the men involved much better than I do. How would you assess them?'

Mevrouw De Boer pursed her lips and clasped her hands in front of herself defensively. 'You must make allowances for the fact that Wolf has lost his wife. There is no moderating female influence in that house.'

'I have heard suggestions that he mistreated her,' I offered tentatively.

'They are not suggestions, they are facts! The poor woman had a dog's life with him, and nobody to defend her. The mayor was utterly spineless.'

Boudewijn opened his mouth to object, then decided better of it.

'Not this mayor,' she added, 'but an earlier one. Not that today's is any better.'

'I understand the man who was minister then had words with him.'

'If he did, much good did it do! She was dead within half a year.'

'A lady's complaint, I believe.'

'If you believe that, you're a bigger fool than he is,' she said, inclining her head towards Boudewijn.

'What, then?'

'It's not proper to describe what he did to her. She bled all right, but not in a natural way. In her last agonies she told mevrouw Hoeks how it had happened. Of course, being a decent woman, mevrouw Hoeks never speaks about it, but I believe she told the mayor of the time, but Wolf explained her allegations away as the ravings of a dying woman.'

'Maybe, then, mevrouw Wolf has received justice at last.'

'Not without an apology. He showed no contrition. You're the learned dominie, but I'd say that she will be feasting with God's chosen ones and he'll be in some other place entirely, never to be reunited with her. At least, if the Almighty knows what He's about.'

Once in a while, without naming names, I recite that speech to my students to ask whether it is proper to question the Almighty's disposition. The answer, I am sure, must be no; but I have lost count of the number of students who tell me that their mothers or grandmothers have expressed similar views.

'And young Joost?'

'His father's son. Neither of them had an ounce of godliness in them. The boy was about fourteen when his mother died, but already he was showing signs of turning into his father. The apple never falls far from the tree, they say. He's a well-built lad, strong, works hard. That much I will say for him. But his tongue is vulgar and he is too fond of his unruly friends in the alehouse. That's the trouble with the young people of today. Indulgent parents! Not that his father didn't curb him from time to time, but how can you expect a boy to grow up knowing right from wrong when his father sets him no fit example?'

'And how would you describe mijnheer Zwart?'

'As different from Wolf as the sun from the moon. Zwart is a family man. His wife is a pretty wee thing — have you met her?'

'Yes, I have,' I admitted. 'It was she who asked me to come here to offer my services.'

'And save her husband's neck, no doubt. Well, you can't blame her. From what I hear, it looks hard to explain things any other way than that Zwart killed Wolf.'

'But is Zwart hot-tempered or fiery?'

'He has his moments. Don't all men, saving your cloth, Master? But he isn't known for brawling or drinking, he's a hard worker and the children are well cared for. That smallholding was run down when he took it on, and now he makes a living from it. Not much more than a living, but it's much better tended than it used to be.'

'I don't suppose that will be true of the Wolfs' farm soon. I didn't get the impression that young Joost has it in him to revive its fortunes,' I said. I did not intend it to come out but I must have said it aloud. That is another of my bad habits.

Mevrouw De Boer was quick to answer. 'His father could only teach him what he knows about farming. The boy cannot learn more than the father knows. So I doubt he will know enough,' she decided, 'because mijnheer Wolf was not a born farmer.'

'He spoke of trying to raise the money for a cow or another pig.'

'Did he?' Mevrouw De Boer inspected the sky. 'It may rain later, but it won't rain silver,' she said.

'Perhaps some kind souls might offer him some charity, given the calamity that has befallen him,' I suggested.

Mevrouw De Boer softened. 'Perhaps. But I'm not sure it would be a kindness. Better if he took the money and used it to set up in another trade. If he can't look after one pig, I don't see how he will do better with two, do you?'

I thanked her for her time and we turned to walk to the Hoeks' house.

'What did you make of that, Boudewijn?' I asked as we strolled.

'I think, Master, that if you're looking for charity that's one door you would not knock on.'

'I'm not so sure. She doesn't want to see money thrown away, but I think if we found something suitable for Joost she would want to support it. Her animosity seemed to me to be largely directed towards his father.'

'He was an easy man to dislike, Master.'

An idea struck me belatedly. 'What about the boys who work there? Could one of them have done it?'

Boudewijn appeared to be ready to deny it at once, then thought better of it. 'They are young, but strong enough, I suppose. But I cannot imagine that mevrouw De Boer is not constantly watching them.'

'She can't when she goes out, Boudewijn, and we've already heard that she left them unsupervised while she and mevrouw Hoeks went to Leiden.'

'That's very true,' Boudewijn commented, looking at me with the degree of respect you might bestow on someone who had delivered themselves of some startling scientific discovery.

'Could we discover their names, Boudewijn?'

'Oh, that's easy, Master. One is my younger brother Gillis, and the other is his friend Gerrit Hoet.'

'Your younger brother?'

'Yes, he's nearly seventeen.'

'If you don't mind my saying so, there must be a big gap between you.'

'There are two other brothers. But he is really my half-brother, Master. We have different mothers.'

'Oh — I'm sorry.'

'What for?'

Now I began to feel awkward. 'I assumed your mother must have died,' I said.

'No, she lives yet,' said Boudewijn. 'She lives with my wife and me.'

'Ah, I see,' I said, even though I did not.

'My mother was very young when she had me,' Boudewijn explained, then dropped his head so as not to look at me. 'That is the shame I always carry.'

It took me a few moments to realise what he meant. 'So your father did not marry your mother.'

'When he knew what had happened, he let her fall like a hot coal. He still denies that I am his, though my mother swears she has never known another man.'

I felt some compassion for Boudewijn. People are so quick to sit in judgement upon children who have no part in the sin that brought them about. Those who think this way are quick to quote four or five passages from the Old Testament that say that God visits the sins of the fathers unto the third or fourth generation; it may be so, but what loving Father punishes those who are not guilty? It seems to me that all the quotations I know on the subject, be they from Exodus, chapter twenty or anywhere else refer to rebellion against God, apostasy from the faith, not any other sin; for in Numbers, chapter fourteen we read "The Lord is long-suffering, and of great mercy, forgiving iniquity and transgression, and by no means clearing the guilty, visiting the iniquity of the fathers upon the sons to the third and fourth generation." But if he forgives iniquity and transgression, how could he visit it upon the descendants? It must be one or the other. It seems clear to me that God forgives those who repent or who do not follow their fathers in iniquity; and Boudewijn had not.

'Your mother never married?'

'Who would have her? Yet she would not reject me, Master. She did not put me away, or foster me in some other family, but brought me up, sometimes in great hardship. She suffered greatly at the tongues of others, as I have myself.' He looked deeply unhappy.

'Are people unkind to you because of your birth, Boudewijn?'

'They sneer at me because I am a bastard. There, I have said it. I know what I am. I did not choose to be such, but it is what I am.'

I looked around. 'Boudewijn, before we go in to mevrouw Hoeks, let us sit upon those tree stumps a moment. I have something to say.'

I said a quick prayer before opening my mouth again. I find my own words are often inadequate, but I needed to get this precisely right.

'Nearly three years ago, Boudewijn, I was in London.'

'London, Master? What were you doing there?'

'I was part of the embassy sent to agree the marriage of the Stadhouder to Princess Mary of England.'

'The Princess? Have you met her?'

'Yes, I did.'

'I hear she is a good woman.'

'She is, Boudewijn, a dutiful daughter to her father and a good niece to her uncle the King.'

'And monstrous tall, I hear?'

'I wouldn't use the word "monstrous", but she is a tall lady.'

'Even taller than the Stadhouder, Master?'

'Let's not worry about that just at the moment, Boudewijn. The point I wanted to make is that the King of England has a number of children by several different women, and nobody treats the children badly as a result. They are not mysteriously tainted by their parents' sin. While there is much in England that would not seem proper to Dutch eyes, that is one respect in which they may be more charitable than we are.'

The Stadhouder was uncomfortable about his compactness, and the discovery that his cousin, the new bride, had grown to be a hand's-breadth taller than he was had not improved his temper, though we had hinted at that fact before they wed. Since then, they had, to some extent, rectified the situation. She wore slippers, and he wore heeled boots, and when they went out of their palaces they tried to be seen sitting down, either in a carriage or on horseback. William was a fine rider, which is ironic because it was a fall from a horse that would lead to his death some time later; but I get ahead of myself again.

Boudewijn sat and thought for a while, and it seemed important that I should let him do so. At length he stood up and brushed himself down. 'Scripture tells us to honour our father and our mother, Master, and I honour my mother for caring for me all my life. Should I honour my father who disowned me? Would God expect that?'

I am not used to questions quite as incisive as that one, certainly not from my undergraduates, many of whom would expect half marks for a near miss if they suggested there were Nine Commandments. 'It seems to me,' I said cautiously, 'that if he does not claim to be your father, he can hardly complain if you do not honour him.'

'I like to think he will be punished in the world to come for the way he treated my mother. Is that wicked of me?'

'I wouldn't say wicked. It might be ungenerous, but it would also be entirely human. However, taking care of our own salvation as best we may is enough for any man or woman. We have no control over how God deals with others, and if He pardons them, who are we to complain? If your father repents of all he has done, he can know his sins will be wiped out.'

Boudewijn was like a dog who is not ready to give up his bone. 'And if I meet my father in Heaven, Master, and I punch him on the nose, will I be cast out for all time?'

I had to smile. 'Boudewijn, if you get to Heaven, as I pray we both will, it will be because you don't want to punch anyone on the nose.'

CHAPTER NINE

We knocked on the door of mijnheer and mevrouw Hoeks.

'I wondered if you were going to come to me,' mevrouw Hoeks said. 'I could see you talking out there in the lane.'

Considering that we had been sitting on a couple of low tree stumps behind another tree I wondered how exactly she had managed to see us there, but I dare say upstairs windows have their uses, if you lean far enough out.

'Well, come in, mijnheer!' she urged.

Boudewijn hesitated.

'I'm sure you know Boudewijn, who is helping me. I am Master Mercurius, of the University of Leiden, and I am assisting the mayor in investigating what happened to mijnheer Wolf.'

Suddenly she seemed a little less eager to speak, though whether this was due to my choice of companion or the subject of my meeting was not immediately clear. 'I'm not sure what I can tell you, but sit down, please. Boudewijn, there's a stool under the window you can use. I'll just fetch my husband Lenaert. He will be keen to meet a minister from Leiden, I'm sure. He's an elder of our church here, you know.'

So saying, she exited through the back door and returned a few minutes later with a ruddy faced man with a wispy grey circlet of hair around his scalp, dirty hands and a long leather apron. He also had filthy clogs which he was ordered to remove before coming into the house, and he was then directed to a bowl to wash his hands before greeting us. My grandmother used to say "The man is head of the family, but the woman is the neck that permits the head to move" and now I knew exactly what she meant. Just because the neck is under the head does not mean it does not control it.

I introduced myself once more.

'Cornelia tells me you are helping to find whoever did this terrible thing to Wolf,' he said.

'Yes, that's right,' I agreed.

'Good thing too. A man should pay the penalty for his misdeeds. If we do not achieve that, then the sin lies upon all of us.'

This is a common opinion amongst people of a Calvinist turn of mind, particularly of the older generation. Sin lies on a community if the individual cannot be identified. I suppose that would make some sense if they made no effort to find the villain, or if they withheld judgment upon him, but otherwise I cannot see that you can blame people for others' offences; but I considered that this was not the time to enter into that argument.

'I should be grateful if your wife would describe what she saw on the day of Wolf's death.'

'Of course she will, won't you, my dear?' Lenaert said.

I doubt mevrouw Hoeks would have held back from giving her account short of an outright prohibition from her husband. She leaned forward and began to recount her memories with relish. 'I had been shopping in Leiden with my friend Gesina de Boer.'

So that was her name! I had been worrying that I might accidentally call her Widow De Boer to her face.

'We made a couple of good bargains and were in happy mood when we returned. There is nothing Gesina likes better than making a good bargain, Master. You'll have seen at the bottom of the lane there's a little dip that sometimes fills with water in wet weather. We had just reached there when we saw Jaco Zwart cross the road ahead of us.'

'Forgive me,' I interrupted, 'which way was he going?'

'Oh, from Wolf's house towards his own.'

'And was he angry or violent?'

She considered this briefly. 'I wouldn't say angry like Wolf gets angry. Got angry, I mean. Vexed, certainly; a bit like my Lenaert when something won't work properly. You won't hear any cursing or yelling, but you know he's smouldering.'

Lenaert wanted to protest, but he could see he would have been overruled.

'Anyway, Wolf came chasing after him and was shouting abuse, but Zwart brushed it away with a gesture. We couldn't hear exactly what was being said, but clearly Wolf wanted Zwart to come to look at something, and I think it was something to do with his pig.'

'I've heard a lot about this pig,' I said, partly to give mevrouw Hoeks a chance to breathe.

'It's a brute,' opined Lenaert. 'Even by the standards of pigs, that one's a bad one. I'll swear he knows he's doing wrong, breaking into other folk's land and trampling their plants, but he still does it.'

'Well, he'll never learn if he's not corrected, will he?' Cornelia expostulated. 'He's just a wild animal who knows nothing of boundaries and properties. He's never been schooled by his owner, so you can't blame the poor animal.'

'He seems to have caused a lot of trouble,' I said.

'I doubt there's a holding this side of town that hasn't had its troubles with Wolf's pig,' Lenaert declared, 'and not many who haven't had a run-in with Wolf neither.'

'I know there's a fancy Latin saying that means you don't speak ill of the dead,' Cornelia began.

'*De mortuis nihil nisi bonum*,' I heard myself saying. I can't resist speaking Latin. 'Or, if you prefer, *De mortuis nil nisi bonum dicendum est.*'

'I knew you'd know,' Cornelia said, 'you being a University man.'

I could have assured her that while almost all the teaching staff would have known it, I doubt that the same was true of all the students. I remember the difficulty I had getting one student to understand that the celebrated Trojan horse was in fact a Greek horse, full of Greeks. There would not have been much point in Trojans going to the trouble of building a large wooden horse they could hide in so that they might enter their own city, but that seemed to be beyond his comprehension.

'Anyway,' Cornelia continued, 'Wolf was a difficult man. There's no gainsaying it.'

'Very difficult,' agreed her husband. 'He'd test any man's charitable heart.'

'I understand he gave his wife a difficult life.'

'Difficult death, more like,' Cornelia growled. 'She wouldn't say anything, but any woman could guess what he'd done to her.'

'What was that?' asked Boudewijn, whose curiosity had finally got the better of him.

'It's not fit for a man's ears,' she said. 'Maybe he didn't intend it, but he caused her death all right. And never showed a minute's remorse for it.'

It seemed a good time to change the subject. 'Mevrouw, did you hear any more after the altercation you described?'

'No, I don't think so. We carried on past the Wolf house to our own.'

'May I ask a question, Master?' asked Boudewijn.

'Of course,' I replied, hoping that he was not going to return to anything that had been discussed earlier.

'Mevrouw, when you passed Wolf's house, did you see whether the pig was in front of the house, or behind?'

'There was nothing to see in front,' she said, and I could be fairly confident that if there had been anything to see, mevrouw Hoeks would have seen it.

Now I felt a fool for not asking before. If Zwart and Wolf had gone round the back of the house, it was harder to explain why Zwart would have stabbed him at the front, in more open view. Admittedly Joost was at the back, but surely if Joost had been watching a continuing argument he would have followed his father to the front? He cannot have known his father was going to be stabbed, but he might well have anticipated a fight, so the fact that he stayed behind the house, by his own admission, must surely mean that he did not anticipate that the argument would turn violent.

Lenaert Hoeks broke the silence. 'When do you expect we can bury Wolf?'

'It is not for me to say, but I think we have discovered all that science can tell us about his death since he has been examined by the Rector of the University.'

Lenaert looked impressed, as if anyone who could be operated upon by the Rector must be a superior type of corpse.

'I will ask the mayor,' said Boudewijn.

'Thank you,' said Lenaert. 'Of course, he had no recent connection with the church, and there may be some that think we should not give space in our graveyard to a notorious evil-liver, but I am an elder of the church and I think we should be forgiving to this poor lost sheep.'

I admit I was a little surprised. I had expected Lenaert Hoeks to be one of those who would dig up an unsuitable corpse and heave it over the wall into the road, but perhaps I had misjudged him.

'We must find him a shroud,' his wife said.

'There will be some in the vestry,' Lenaert told her, patting her reassuringly on the hand. 'We keep some for the use of any paupers who die here.'

I was pleased to hear it, but I confess that I had never thought who would shroud the poor. Every person I have ever buried was decently dressed; not that I have much experience, because I was only called upon when the minister of the Hooglandse Kerk went for a holiday.

'Have you met our minister, Master?' Lenaert asked me.

'No, I haven't had that pleasure yet,' I said.

'He's a good man, quite a young man. Very learned, in his way,' Lenaert said. 'But I think he misses the city. It wouldn't surprise me if he decided he was being called to serve elsewhere before long. Then we shall have a vacancy, I suppose.'

He left that thought hanging in the air; and so did I. I did not want to serve in a country parish, or any kind of parish, but to say so might have soured relationships here.

Unfortunately, the comment had not escaped Boudewijn.

'The minister would much rather be in Leiden or The Hague, I think, Master. He serves us well enough, of course, but it is a quiet place and I suspect he feels cut off from other men of the cloth.'

I refrained from pointing out that he only had to walk less than an hour into the city and he would have had the company of forty or fifty of them, many of them my colleagues in the

Faculty of Theology. Not that we are all good company; I cannot remember a time when all the staff have been speaking to each other. There always seems to be a doctrinal dispute of some kind going on.

'Boudewijn, that is a decision that the minister must make for himself in his own time. We all feel separated from our brethren occasionally.'

That is one of the burdens of being a secret Catholic priest. It may be that I pass by another every day; or perhaps there is no other in the southern half of Holland. I cannot know. There are days when I wonder how I can maintain my own orthodoxy with little or no contact with others. I maintain good relationships with a couple of open priests, but not in Leiden. It would be too risky. I dare not say who they were even now, for fear that they will be persecuted for not having exposed me. I doubt they are alive; but then they probably doubt whether I am alive too.

'I think we can fit one more interview in before I have to return to Leiden. Who is next?' I asked.

'Jan and Griet Smulders, Master. You'll recall I warned you that Jan likes the tavern.'

'Yes, I remember that.'

The door was answered by mevrouw Smulders, who called to her husband who was clearing a patch of earth in the kitchen garden. He showed none of the usual signs of heavy drinking, and I began to wonder if his alleged fondness for the tavern was actually one for lively company.

I introduced myself and explained our mission. 'I was hoping you might be able to give me some information about mijnheer Wolf. Did he have any enemies?'

Jan snorted. 'I'll make you a list of his friends. It'll be quicker for us both,' he said.

'He was not a popular man, then?'

'As popular as foot-rot,' Jan replied.

'Come now,' his wife interjected, 'when he first came here, things were different.'

This sounded interesting. 'Please tell me about your first impressions,' I said.

'You see, Master, Wolf wasn't born hereabouts,' said Griet. 'The smallholding belonged to his uncle, his mother's brother. When he died, his children having all gone before him, he bequeathed it to his sister, who sent Wolf to tend it. It had been neglected, what with his uncle not having been a well man for some time before he died. I think she had it in mind to pretty it up and then sell it on. But Franciscus took to it. Jan here lent a hand, and it was looking much tidier within a six-month.'

'We all helped where we could,' Jan explained. 'That's what you do around here. If someone needs a bit of assistance, you all muck in.'

'So Franciscus thought he would keep it, the country air agreeing with him and, I think, a little distance between a grown man and his mother is a healthy thing. It's natural for a grown child to want their own home. The trouble was he hadn't been bred to it.'

'What my wife really means, dominie, is that he wouldn't listen to anyone. He had his own ideas about what he would grow and how, and they didn't work. There's a reason we don't grow corn here. The soil's too heavy and it holds too much water, but he wouldn't listen. And in no time he'd run out of money and was begging the loan of seed. You'll remember eight summers back we had the worst of the war, and it ruined many a farmer. I didn't think he would come back from that, but give him his due, he kept trying. But he never managed to earn enough in the summer to set himself up well for the next spring. So he thought he'd give pig farming a try and bought that creature he has now.'

'Like master, like beast, Master,' Griet chipped in.

'He's an unruly animal, I'll grant,' Jan continued. 'But he's never been trained. He roams where he wants, and so long as he comes back in the evening Wolf didn't care. He did no end of damage to other people's properties, but there was no point taxing Wolf about it, because he hadn't two stuivers to rub together anyway.'

'I heard he was married…' I prompted, setting Griet off on a spasm of tutting.

'He was, Master, and to a nice girl too. Elisabeth, her name was, from a family out Koudekerk way.'

I knew Koudekerk aan den Rijn. It was a village to the south-east of Leiden, perhaps two hours' walk.

'I dread to think what her poor parents thought when they realised what their daughter had gone through. It was all good at first. Little Joost soon turned up and that was while Franciscus still had his grand plans, but as they turned sour, so did he. We'd notice there were some Sundays when she wasn't at church. Then he stopped going too. We heard he'd fallen out with the old minister about her. I'm sure he meant well, Master, but the minister's intervention didn't serve Elisabeth well at all. She took some fearful beatings. You tried to talk to him about it, didn't you?' she nudged Jan.

'I did, us being just a bit older, but he didn't take kindly to it. Accused me of interfering between a man and his wife and said I'd probably got my eye on her for myself, because Griet wasn't enough for me. He said if he found Elisabeth was sweet on me, he'd know what to do about it. I swear there was nothing of that sort, Master. All I did was to remind him that the Good Book says "Husband, love thy wife!" and he was deaf to that. He said he used her as she deserved to be used, but I reckon she was blameless. She was just something to take out his passions on, just a thing to him. It was pitiful.'

'Then she took sick and died,' Griet added, and I could see tears forming in the corners of her eyes and running down her cheeks as she said it. 'It was a miserable end, too. It comes to us all, I know, but we can hope for it to be in our own bed with our family there and the invisible angels waiting to take us. She had her boy there, but she died in great pain. I heard one of her howls, Master, and hope never to hear the like again. Of course, we all wanted to help but he'd not admit any of us to the house.'

'And this was about six years ago?' I prompted gently.

'The last day of April, 1674,' Griet said. 'A Monday. She'd been very poorly for about a week, and I thought maybe I could go into her when Franciscus and Joost were at church, so I didn't go to church that Sunday, but they never set foot outside the gate either. I saw Joost in the back field and called across to him to see how his mother did, but he just said she was fading fast, so I asked if she needed anything. And you know what he said? "A miracle", he said. Just that. A miracle.'

'Now, don't upset yourself, my dear,' Jan comforted her, taking her hand in his.

'It wasn't right,' Griet protested. 'A woman's lot is often pain, but there's enough of it without her man adding to it. I'm not a vindictive woman, Master, honestly I'm not, but I could hope Our Father is dealing sharply with Franciscus now. And I hope and believe that Elisabeth is free from suffering and enjoying Paradise. Am I wrong to think that?'

I hate this kind of question. As a Reformed minister, I must teach that God selects a few for eternal bliss and the rest are separated from Him; as a Catholic priest, I can believe that there are those whose unmerited suffering qualifies them to be called saints. But the question of eternal punishment is not susceptible to easy answers. Consider, for a moment, how awful punishment without hope of an end must be, and how very sincerely those miscreants must repent of their misdoings. Is God entirely deaf to their pleas? Think of my brother Laurentius, killed in battle nearly fifteen years earlier. Laurentius was a good man, an honest man. I doubt that his soul was burdened by any great sins, but did he have time to repent before he was taken? Can it really be that because he died on Saturday he was damned, whereas if he had lived till Sunday he would have been saved?

I put these thoughts aside and prepared to answer Griet. Fortunately, when you're a minister people assume if you dither about answering it's because you're praying. 'You think what your decency tells you to think, mevrouw. You believe that God is just, and therefore the suffering are rewarded and the wicked are punished. That is the only conclusion our knowledge of God will support. It is not vindictive to expect God to be God.'

Jan was deep in thought. 'So tell me, Master, is it a bad thing to murder a murderer? After all, we'll do it on the scaffold sooner or later.'

This couple were doing a good job of finding my least favourite questions. I do not like the idea that by finding a villain I am contributing to their death. The Commandment instructs us not to kill; there are no footnotes beginning "except…" that I know of. 'The Lord says vengeance is his, mijnheer.'

Lo and behold, Boudewijn decided to join in. 'So, Master, answer me this. If I see a man about to stab mijnheer Smulders and I quickly draw my sword and run him through, I'll be accounted a hero and nobody will criticise me. But if I arrive five minutes later, when mijnheer Smulders is dead, and I do exactly the same thing, I'm described as a murderer, unless he offered violence to me. Is that right?'

'I believe it is what the law says, Boudewijn. As to whether it is right, the best guide is your conscience. Would you feel confident about standing before the Almighty and saying that you did this deed and you believe it was right to do so?'

'I would, Master; but I'm asking if I'm wrong.'

'I think every faith holds that saving life is a sacred duty, so killing an assailant to achieve that is permitted; killing an assailant later, when life has already been lost, is not.'

'Well said, Master!' exclaimed Jan Smulders. 'Good, clear, Godly teaching!'

It was time to bring us all back to the point. 'Did either of you hear or see anything that passed between mijnheer Zwart and mijnheer Wolf on the day of the killing?'

'Not with my own ears,' Griet answered. 'Gesina de Boer told me what had passed, but I can't say I heard it.'

'Nor I,' agreed Jan. 'I was in the back, as I was today.'

'Did you see Joost?'

'Aye, on and off. He came and went a few times. But I didn't hear a fight, if that's what you mean, and the first I knew of it was when Joost was running up and down the lane shouting for help. We went running — the men, that is — but Wolf was gone.'

'And did Joost accuse anyone?'

'Not at the time. He seemed dumbstruck. It was only when we had confirmed that his father was dead that he said Jaco killed him and said he must go to the mayor to denounce him.'

'And did you go with him?'

'Yes. We could do nothing for Franciscus except cover him, and Joost was like a wild thing. We feared for his reason.'

I thanked them for their help and we took our leave.

'That's as much as we can do today, Boudewijn. I must return to Leiden before nightfall. I'll come again tomorrow.'

'Can I come with you, Master? This inquisiting is exciting.'

'Is it? For me it's a burden, Boudewijn.'

'Then why do you do it?'

'Sometimes, because I have no choice. I'm ordered to do so by those above me. Sometimes because compassion tells me the victim needs the truth to be found. Sometimes because I believe someone has been wrongly accused.'

'Is that what you feel here, Master?'

I thought hard before answering — for once. 'I thought so, Boudewijn, but I'm not sure. I really don't know who killed Franciscus Wolf.'

CHAPTER TEN

The following morning was, if anything, even colder. Having ventured outside the door, I swiftly returned to my chamber to don an extra shirt and a pair of thick gloves. I also wrapped my feet in cloth to keep them dry and warm inside my boots. Sadly, the extra thicknesses prevented my getting the boots on, so I had to remove layers like peeling an onion until my feet would fit.

I have read that in the far north there are animals made to suit their wintry home. They have white fur so as not to be seen, and I have seen the skin of one like a large deer that can keep its feet on the ice. I have no such gift. You will not see me skating on frozen ponds, and I trudge through snow. We once had a man from Sweden at the University who moved around in snow by fixing planks of wood to his boots and paddling with sticks. He told us all his compatriots learned to do so when they were small and they were wonderfully adept with these planks, sliding down hills at great speed and weaving through the trees. It is a wonder that Swedish forests are not littered with the corpses of these fools.

The fresh snow slowed my progress, and by the time I arrived at Oegstgeest I was quite weary and my feet were frozen, so I gladly accepted Boudewijn's invitation to sit by the pot-bellied stove and dry my boots while I sipped gratefully at a goblet of hot, spiced wine and tried to find good reasons not to go back out again.

'Master,' said Boudewijn, 'may I ask how you became an inquisitor?'

'It's a long story,' I said, but he showed no sign of changing the subject, so I continued. 'I started in 1671, when the mayor of Delft asked the University for help in finding the abductor of three little girls.'

Boudewijn goggled. 'Three girls?'

'Yes. A weaver's daughter, the daughter of a fish-seller and the daughter of a rich merchant.'

'And the University sent you?'

'Yes. Don't ask me why, but the Rector thought I was the best man to send. I suppose some of the professors were too old and one or two were not very practical.'

I felt a twinge of conscience in saying this, because I am not very worldly myself; but I am entitled to a certain feeling that I am not quite as impractical as some. There is a lecturer who teaches Greek who must need help dressing himself in the morning.

'And did you find the kidnapper?'

'Yes, eventually.'

'Eventually? How long did it take, Master?'

'About a week, I think.'

Boudewijn fell silent for a while. 'I pray we'll find the killer of mijnheer Wolf within a week,' he finally said.

'Amen to that,' I replied.

'But how can we do it, Master? Surely whoever killed Wolf made sure that there were no witnesses?'

'I'm afraid we keep asking the same questions of as many people as possible. At some point there will be a contradiction and then we have to test which account is to be preferred. Alternatively, we may discover a reason for killing Wolf that points to one person.'

'It sounded to me as if everyone had a reason for killing Wolf, Master. Nobody had a good word for him.'

'Perhaps, Boudewijn. But they did not, in fact, all kill him. And, on the assumption that we are not dealing with a lunatic who might kill without reason, the murderer had a reason to kill; and we may even say that there is a reason why it was done then, and not at another time. The neighbours all disliked him, but they had disliked him for years. Why kill him now? The more I think about it, the more I think that is where the solution will have to be found.'

The arrival of the mayor caused our conversation to be interrupted and we separated, Boudewijn to return to his day job while I followed the mayor into his office to describe our progress.

'I have spoken to a number of people,' I explained. 'Zwart, of course, and also Joost Wolf. He is hopeful that there may be some charitable relief that will enable him to buy another animal and build up the farm once more.'

The mayor looked doubtful. 'That won't be easy. This is not a town where we have a lot of comfortable men with spare money to give. There is not much difference between the highest and the lowest here. That is not to say that they are not public-spirited, but their capacity to help may be limited. And, to be frank, given that much of mijnheer Wolf's substance was wasted in the alehouse, there may be reluctance to replace it.'

'Perhaps the alehouse keeper is the first person to ask, then,' I proposed.

The mayor smiled ruefully. 'He's probably the wealthiest man in Oegstgeest, more's the pity.'

'Unfortunately, Joost cannot tell us much. He was at the back of the house and did not realise that the confrontation had flared up once more until he heard a noise, presumably his father falling on the ground. He ran into the road and met the two women. Gesina de Boer and Cornelia Hoeks, who were just returning from a shopping trip to Leiden.'

'And did they have anything useful to add?'

'Not really. They saw Jaco Zwart walking away, but he was not hurrying as one might expect. The chief matter of interest in their testimonies was a clear antipathy to Franciscus Wolf. There seems to be a widespread belief that he was responsible for the death of his wife.'

'There is,' said the mayor, 'and I share it. Wolf never directly denied it, but he argued that it was nobody's business but his what went on in his household. Sadly, mevrouw Wolf believed the same, and gave very little information to anyone outside that might have incriminated her husband. You will have heard, I assume, that the previous minister taxed Wolf after an earlier incident?'

'Yes. I understand his intervention was badly received.'

'You could put it like that. Wolf threw the minister out of his house and stopped going to church. I'm afraid the minister did not handle it well, because he began by agreeing that nobody had authority to question Wolf's actions except Wolf himself, so he tried to appeal to Wolf's sense of self-discipline. And he had none.'

'Was mevrouw Wolf's body examined after her death to determine the cause?'

The mayor looked distinctly uneasy. 'If it was, I heard nothing about it. So far as I recall, the mayor of the time thought that since she died of a fever it could not be connected with any maltreatment meted out by her husband. It wasn't until after she was buried that her family produced a surgeon who affirmed that the fever might be the result of festering of a wound.'

'Why did the family delay?'

'That's simple. Because Wolf didn't tell them she was dead. I was surprised that there was nobody from her home village at the funeral, but then we found out why. Our minister was moved to go there one day to consult his fellow minister, and together they told the family, such as was left. I think her father had died, but she had a mother, brothers and a sister still living then.'

This was shocking news. Here was a potential suspect with ample reason to wreak revenge on Wolf. 'And are they still alive?'

'I don't know,' admitted the mayor. 'But perhaps we should find out.'

'It's not the anniversary of her death, because that was in April, but I wonder what would cause someone to take revenge six years later?'

'Maybe her birthday or some such event? If you're going to go today, we'll have to hire you a horse. It's quite a way off, especially in this weather.'

'Thank you, but I want to speak to the other families today. Perhaps I could go to Koudekerk tomorrow?'

'As you wish, Master. I place myself in your hands. But if you do, why not stay the night at my house again, and ride from here in the morning?'

'I could not impose…' I began, rather half-heartedly, because the prospect of another evening in the company of young Joanna Gerrits was already banishing the winter chill.

'Nonsense! We would be honoured. So that's settled,' he concluded, without giving me the opportunity of demurral.

I stammered my thanks and returned to my review of the previous day. 'I also visited Jan and Griet Smulders. Mevrouw

Smulders described what she knew of Elisabeth's last day of life.'

'They're good people,' the mayor announced. 'In fact, I'd have said everyone there was, except Wolf. Of course, the Pijls have the disadvantage of being Roman Catholics, but they are sober and reliable despite that.'

'I was told Jan Smulders was a drinker, but I saw little evidence of it.'

The mayor shrugged. 'He drinks a bit, but that isn't why he goes to the alehouse. Mijnheer Smulders likes a sing-song, and he isn't going to get that at home. His wife has strong views about that kind of thing, not to mention having a voice like a chicken having its neck wrung. If he wants to sing in company, the alehouse is his best option. Mind you, I've never heard him sing anything low or unbecoming.'

'Is the mayor of those days still alive?'

'He is, but only from the neck down, I'm afraid. He's become a little infantile, and I doubt you'd get much sense from him. He suffered a lot of criticism at the time, some merited, some unfair, but it soured his enjoyment of the office and he retired from all public life after his term. It seemed to prey on him and he became addled. I could take you to him, but I think his daughter would much rather we didn't turn that rock over, if you see what I mean.'

'Of course,' I agreed. I could imagine how such events could unnerve even the strongest of men.

The mayor stood up. 'I'm keeping you from your enquiries,' he said. 'Do you want Boudewijn again today?'

'If I may. He's very useful at assuring people that I am here with your consent.'

'To be frank,' said the mayor, 'I was uncertain at first. No reflection on you, of course, but I couldn't put such a matter into just anyone's hands. Now I can see that you were sent by God to lead us through this. And, equally frankly, in view of what happened to my poor predecessor, I am pleased to be relieved of the burden.'

'Your brother and his friend,' I said to Boudewijn. 'We should talk to them sometime.'

'They could meet us at the end of the day, I'm sure, Master. Perhaps before you go to the mayor's house for dinner.'

I wanted to know how he knew I was doing that, but I imagine the door must have been open; or perhaps it has an unusually large keyhole.

'I'll run ahead and arrange it with them,' Boudewijn announced, and skipped off over the snow as I gingerly picked my way over new ice, slushy puddles and treacherous cavities.

Boudewijn met me again at the first house we came to, that of Matthaeus and Hanna Pijl.

As we approached the door, he whispered urgently to me. 'Don't forget to be on your guard, Master. Remember they're Roman Catholics.'

I wanted to whisper back "So am I" and kid him that we Catholics might seize him and bake him in a pie, but there was just a chance that he might have believed it. People have been accused of stupider things, especially if they were Jews. And, of course, one mention of it in Leiden and I was unlikely to keep my job.

Unusually, Hanna Pijl did not immediately fetch her husband, but invited us inside and sat opposite us. One look at the wall demonstrated that we were in a Catholic house. There was devotional art and a crucifix there. Mevrouw Pijl sat patiently with her hands folded in her lap, her blue eyes fixed on me. Even by the standards of Dutch women, she was astonishingly clean. Her cap looked like a dove perched on her head.

'I wonder whether you heard or saw anything on the day that Franciscus Wolf died,' I began.

She crossed herself at the mention of his death. 'I heard Joost running up and down the road and went out to him, but that is all.'

I thought a moment. 'He must have come well up the lane,' I said. 'It's a little way to his home.'

'He was uncommonly loud, Master. He wanted us to seize mijnheer Zwart, whom he accused of doing his father to death.'

'Did he say why he suspected this?'

'He did. My husband asked why he thought that Jaco had anything to do with it, and he replied that the two men had had violent and unseemly words just a few minutes before.'

'But he did not say that he saw anything himself?'

'No. It seemed rather that he could not think of anyone else it could have been.'

'And may I ask whether you thought mijnheer Zwart would be capable of such a thing?'

She remained composed, which gave her words even more of a chilling effect on me. 'I think any of us is capable of anything, if we submit to our passions, Master.'

'Let me then put my question rather differently. Have you ever seen Zwart behave in a manner that led you to think he might be dangerous to others?'

'No, I have not.'

'What did you make of mijnheer Wolf?'

'We had little to do with him.'

'Yet you are neighbours.'

'Yes, but we tried to keep out of company with him. My mother used to tell us that if you pick up dung in lace gloves, the gloves won't affect the dung. It's always the other way round.'

There was no rancour or spleen about Hanna Pijl. She answered calmly and quietly, with a gentle assurance of the rightness of what she was saying.

'Do you know anything of the death of mevrouw Wolf?'

'Only that it happened before we came. We have been here a little over four years, having come at Christmas, 1675.'

'I see. It was not discussed in your hearing, then?'

'I do not listen to gossip, Master. Nor do the other wives here try to engage me in it.'

The room fell quiet. I could think of nothing more to ask, and was about to take my leave and ask to speak to her husband when I noticed a small candle burning. 'Forgive me, mevrouw. Are you remembering someone?'

'I lit a candle for the repose of mijnheer Wolf's soul. Somebody should offer prayers for him. Perhaps since you are here…'

This was more treacherous than you might think. As a Reformed minister, I should tell her that prayers for the dead are an idle Catholic superstition, and that when a person dies his soul goes either to Heaven or Hell. There is no second chance after death. On the other hand, as a Catholic priest I believe that prayers for the dead are an ancient Christian practice, and that such prayers may ease the soul in Purgatory (which, as a Reformed minister, I can't believe in).

'Boudewijn,' I said, 'would you be kind enough to find mijnheer Pijl and ask him if I may come to speak with him in a few minutes?'

'Of course, Master,' said Boudewijn, who seemed to relish the opportunity not to see any extra prayers.

When he was gone, I knelt with mevrouw Pijl and said the prayer in commemoration of the faithful departed. 'Remember, O Lord, Thy servant Franciscus, who has gone before us with the sign of faith, and sleeps the sleep of peace.'

If Hanna Pijl did not realise I was a Catholic before, she might have done then, and as we rose she murmured, 'Thank you,' and held her finger across her lips in token of her silence.

CHAPTER ELEVEN

We walked out into the field behind the house where Matthaeus Pijl was talking over the wall to Piet Aelter. The path to Aelter's large field ran along the side of Pijl's land and, as had been described to me before by Boudewijn, that field abutted Wolf's land at its lower end.

I introduced myself and explained once again that Boudewijn was assisting me. Aelter's face betrayed his concern that Boudewijn could never be of real assistance to anyone, but he said nothing.

'It's a bad business, Master,' Pijl remarked.

'I understand that mijnheer Wolf was not a popular man,' I began tentatively.

'You understand right,' said Aelter forcefully. 'I don't mind saying I've had a set-to with him a few times.' He pointed to the end of the lane where it entered his field. 'The far side of the field doesn't have a fence or hedge, you see. Mainly, it's marked by the stream, and we can't fence it or the animals wouldn't be able to get a drink there. But there's a portion to the right where the stream disappears under a hummock and then dribbles out across the road, and it's marked by boundary stones. From time to time, Master, those stones apparently take it upon themselves to walk up this way a bit. Wolf always said it had nothing to do with him, but he's the only one as would benefit from it, so I always thought it was crystal clear where the blame must lie.'

'Then there's his confounded pig,' Pijl added. 'He doesn't trouble me too much because he doesn't like the thorn bushes I have, though I've caught him once or twice making for my cabbages and had to take a stick to his snout. But he's done some fearful damage to Piet's crops.'

Piet Aelter sucked on a clay pipe he produced from his jacket. 'I can't say I'd have been sorry if it had been the pig that was killed,' he admitted, 'and while it's wicked to speak ill of the dead, I can't say I'm surprised that someone had finally had enough of Wolf.'

Aelter was a tall, spare man, his brown hair flying in all directions around his lined and grooved face from which clear grey eyes looked me up and down. His pipe was unlit, but it seemed to be the sucking of it that helped him think. I would have placed him at around fifty years old.

'Do you live alone here, mijnheer Aelter?'

'Aye, Master, since my wife died three years or more ago. People urge me to take a new wife, but to be honest I haven't the inclination. She was a good wife to me and there won't be her equal, so why bother to look for one?'

'She was a fine woman,' agreed Matthaeus Pijl, 'not that my Hanna isn't too.'

'She is, Master,' Aelter concurred. 'Very kind to me too. When she's laundering, she calls to me to bring my bits to her copper and does them for me. She has no call to be doing that, but it's very much appreciated.' He looked at me belligerently. 'Saving your cloth, dominie, I know they're Romanists but they're good people, and if there's no place for them in Heaven I don't know that I'd want to go there.'

I could not resist a smile. If Catholics are barred from Heaven, that would put me in a difficult position. 'I think, mijnheer Aelter, that I have no better idea than you as to whom God will admit and whom He will not. But I am sure that such acts of charity can only benefit those who perform them.'

Aelter seemed satisfied with this suggestion. 'You might have an argument about that with our local minister, Master, who has no time for the likes of Matthaeus and Hanna.'

'I haven't had the pleasure of meeting him yet,' I answered, 'but I suppose there may be other things we don't agree about.'

Aelter sucked on his pipe. 'He's a young man, about your age, I should think, full of book learning, no doubt, but he doesn't understand people hereabouts. We're not townies, and we don't think like they think. I'll give you an example — when the harvest is to come in, we have to work fast while the weather is good, and that may mean we have to labour on the Sabbath. The old minister understood that, but the new one won't have it. If I don't work, and there are a few days of heavy rain, it may spoil the crop, and then where would I be? The old minister used to have a prayer hour in the evening at Harvest-tide for those who missed the Sunday. It was much appreciated, but it's a thing of the past now.'

I understood his view. There have always been those who must work on the Lord's Day; sailors, for example, cannot stop manning the sails simply because it is Sunday, and cows need milking every day. However, I needed to bring them back to the matter in hand. 'Did either of you see anything untoward on the day Franciscus Wolf died?'

'No, Master,' Aelter answered.

'Me neither,' said Pijl. 'The snag is that from here you can't see either the rear or front of Wolf's house.'

'But noise carries. Did you hear the argument?'

'I didn't.' Pijl was emphatic. 'Did you, Piet?'

'No. I heard the pig squeal louder than normal. Maybe that was when it happened, because a few minutes later you could hear young Joost shouting for help, but I didn't hear either Zwart's or Wolf's voice raised.'

'I heard Joost calling for help,' Pijl agreed, 'and of course I went out to the road to see what it was all about, but by then the women had got there.'

'And did you see mijnheer Wolf before he died?'

Pijl shook his head. 'He was gone before I got there, and I'm quicker than Piet here.'

'You didn't have so far to run either,' Aelter objected.

I had an uneasy feeling about this. Why had Wolf died so quickly? A single stab wound, however dangerous, usually takes a minute or two to cause enough loss of blood to cause the victim to swoon and fall, and then death follows. It was just about possible that if people did not respond immediately, Wolf might have bled to death before they got there, but there was no great puddle of blood on the path. He seemed to have died where he fell, with no attempt to move into the house.

'When you saw Wolf,' I asked, 'can you describe his position?'

Pijl answered first. 'He was lying on the path to his house, his head towards the road. On his back, with his hands close to his chest.'

'But the knife was not there?'

'No, not at all. Blood had been spurting out of the wound with each heartbeat, but soon that dropped to a trickle and he was gone.'

'That's very odd. You see, Wolf cut his hands trying to pull the blade out of his chest. He therefore lived for a while after the stabbing, but he did not shout for help himself, nor was the blade anywhere near, so presumably the killer pulled it out and took it away with him. If it was Zwart, several hours had passed before anyone went to accuse him. Did Wolf say anything about who attacked him?'

'If he did,' Aelter replied, 'the only person who would know would be Joost. As we said, Wolf was past speaking by the time we got there.'

'Joost didn't mention it. You'd think a dying man would tell who had attacked him.'

'But Master,' Pijl objected, 'he bled so fast I doubt he was able to talk at all. And I imagine that when a man knows he's about to die, his first thought is to make his peace with God if he can, in the few moments that are left to him.'

That was true enough. Perhaps I was overcomplicating a very brief episode. A man is stabbed, he falls, he dies; dying declarations and accusations against another are not likely at such a time.

I have seen so little of violent death maybe I just did not know enough to maintain an opinion on what might have happened; and, if the truth be told, I didn't want to be educated. I am a lecturer in moral philosophy; I do not expect to encounter brutal homicide in my day to day work.

I thanked them for their time and Boudewijn and I walked back out to the road, this time along Aelter's path so we came out at a point around the corner from where we had gone in at Pijl's gate.

'They seem honest men,' I said, as much to make conversation as with any piercing insight.

'I believe they are, Master,' Boudewijn concurred.

'Where shall we go next? The house nearest the Zwarts', I think.'

'Abraham and Trijntje Venstra, Master, and their children.'

The Venstras were probably my age or maybe a little less, since their four children were all small, the oldest being only nine. Abraham asked to be excused, explaining that he had to take fodder to the animals, but Boudewijn immediately volunteered that we would help if we could talk as we worked. I had not the heart to say that he was only speaking for himself, so I made to pick up a sheaf of hay.

'You'll dirty your robe, Master,' said Venstra. 'But you could oblige by securing the gate behind us. I don't want Wolf's pig around here again.'

'You've had trouble with him too, then?' I asked.

Venstra laughed, turning to face me as he marched along with an enormous bale of hay on his shoulder. 'I doubt you'll find anyone who hasn't around here. That pig could do with a good sermon on the Ten Commandments.'

Boudewijn appeared shocked that anyone would joke like that in front of a minister.

'And what about Wolf himself?' I asked.

'Franciscus? You take him how you find him. He wasn't a man whose company I would seek, but you knew where you stood with him.'

'Really?' I said, surprised at this positive assessment.

'Oh, yes,' said Venstra. 'You knew he would always behave badly, so you were never taken off guard by what he did.'

'How long have you been here, mijnheer Venstra?'

Venstra paused to do some counting on his fingers. 'It must be coming up to six years. My wife's uncle lives next door, and he told us this small farm was available to rent just after our second was born. I was working as a labourer then, and we wanted the chance to get more space.' He pointed to a wooden platform at the back of his house. 'The children keep coming, so we need more again. I'm building another room there. My wife and I will move in there, and the two girls will have our room. The boys can stay where they are.'

To one whose building skills are non-existent, even building a level platform seems a major achievement, and I was impressed. 'There must be a lot of work there,' I said.

Venstra shrugged. 'Uncle Wim is giving me a hand. He's a better carpenter than I am. We just have to saw some planks and build a wooden box.'

I was fairly sure that there was more to housebuilding than that, but I did not choose to reveal my ignorance. 'On the day that Wolf was killed, did you see or hear anything?'

'Not that I recall. You don't tend to hear much in the house with the noise four children make. I heard Joost shouting for help, but I understand that was after his father had been killed.'

'And did you go to his aid?'

'Not immediately, for two reasons. I wasn't sure what he was shouting at first, and then I needed to finish penning the animals. You can't leave them half in and half out. It was getting towards dusk, and I didn't want to have to round them up in the dark.'

'And how do you find mijnheer Zwart?'

'Jaco? An honest man, a good man. If he killed Wolf, I'm a worse judge of character than even Trijntje tells me I am.'

'Does he have a temper?'

'I've never seen it. In some ways that's harder to read, because I've seen him annoyed, but he doesn't flare up like most. When he told Wolf he'd deal with his pig if he came into his land again, he came to tell me what had been said because he wanted us to present a united front to Wolf. I could see he was annoyed, but he didn't raise his voice. He just said firmly it had to stop.'

'And how do you think Joost will cope?' I asked.

Venstra stopped working, removed his cap and tousled his hair. 'He's not made for farm work. He needs someone to help him, like Uncle Wim helped me when I started here. But I don't think that farm will keep two men comfortably. There's a lot that needs doing to make it productive again. Wolf ran it down through neglect.'

'He has a few goats, I see.'

'Yes, and they give milk. But his reason for having goats was that they'll eat almost anything and they don't need much care. There's not a big market for goat's milk, and he doesn't make cheese. Now that's something I would be trying.'

'Aren't there plenty of cheesemakers nearby?'

'Master, if you make cheese with one type of milk, you can't easily start with another. You have to clean all your vessels thoroughly. The principles are the same, but goat's milk has a strong taste. If you want to go back to making cow's milk cheese afterwards, you need to make sure there's no goat's curds left to taint it, or people will taste them. There are districts where there's a great demand for goat's cheese, but I don't know that I've seen it often in the markets here.'

'Maybe if people sold it regularly, you'd find a market,' suggested Boudewijn.

'Maybe,' conceded Venstra with a grin. 'But if you have a family to feed, are you going to take that chance?'

I could see no point in prolonging our discussion. Venstra clearly had nothing more useful to tell me. 'If I may speak to your wife, I'll ask her the same questions.'

'Please do. You know where you'll find her.'

Some men would take offence at their wives being questioned in their absence, but Venstra seemed to me to be a co-operative and honest man, a good family man. I thanked him for his help, and retraced my steps to the house, where mevrouw Venstra was attempting to get food inside an infant rather than, as the child seemed to want, all over its hair.

'Hands down, Nico!' she was saying as we entered, while the infant waved his arms around trying to intercept the small horn spoon that had been dipped in the egg.

To my surprise, Boudewijn immediately sat himself opposite them and offered the child his index finger, which little Nico grabbed with both hands.

'That's it! You pull and I'll pull,' said Boudewijn, 'but you'll need your egg to make you big and strong.'

Trijntje Venstra offered a tentative spoonful, which Nico slurped up with alacrity.

'Harder! Pull harder!' urged Boudewijn. 'My finger is getting away.'

Nico gurgled with delight, scoffed a big spoonful of egg and returned to the battle against the invading finger.

In no time the egg was gone, the majority of it inside Nico, and the exhausted finger collapsed on Nico's lap.

'You win,' announced Boudewijn. 'Look, my finger needs to rest now.'

Trijntje smiled. 'Thank you,' she said to Boudewijn. 'It's a battle every mealtime.'

'My wife's mother taught me that trick,' he replied.

'I won't keep you,' I said. 'I can see you're very busy. I just wanted to ask a few questions.'

'Of course, Master. It is our Christian duty to help you.'

I would not have dared to say that, but neither would I argue with her. It was a belief likely to lead to greater co-operation than I was used to. 'Tell me, mevrouw, did you see or hear anything when Wolf was killed?'

Trijntje shook her head vigorously. 'Nothing, Master. Not until Abraham came in from the field behind and asked me if I had heard shouting. But I'm afraid when these little ones become excited, it's hard to hear anything outside.'

To demonstrate the point, Nico began beating the spoon on the table while simultaneously shouting "Bam, bam, bam". Very quickly I could hear nothing else. During a brief interval I managed to squeeze in one more question. 'Can you tell me what manner of man you found Wolf to be?'

Trijntje shuddered. 'I did not like him, Master. He never talked to me, only to my husband. I suppose you might say he was a man's man, but it seemed to me that he had no interest in what a woman might have to say. Abraham isn't like that. While I hope I am an obedient wife, he does not walk over me. If Abraham asks me something, it is because he wants my answer. And there are some things where he will defer to me. If I say that a child is sick and needs an apothecary, Abraham never wants to argue with me. He gives me whatever money we can spare to go to one.'

'Is there one in Oegstgeest?' I asked.

'Not a properly trained one,' Boudewijn interrupted. 'If it's at all possible, we'll walk into Leiden and seek one out there. It's not cheap but when a child is sick, you want the best you can get.'

'You wouldn't go to a physician?'

'If money fell like rain I would,' Trijntje told us, 'but people like us can't afford physicians. We find an apothecary or, if we have no money, we may ask at the Begijnhof.'

The begijns are women who choose to live rather like nuns, though they take no lifelong vows. They devote themselves to prayer and good works. I could well imagine the poor asking there for help. Some of the begijns may well be mothers themselves; widowed women with adult children might choose to enter there rather than marry again. At any event, you would find a sympathetic ear, and, in common with many institutions in Leiden, no questions were asked about your own denomination.

'And Joost?' I asked. 'How would you describe him?'

Trijntje seemed perturbed by my question. 'He is a confused young man. The only example he has in his life is his father, so he has never learned to speak respectfully to women. If ever I have to deal with him he just says what he has to say, then he leaves. He often doesn't look me in the eye. I don't think he's a bad boy, but he doesn't know what makes for a good boy.'

'He lost his mother some time ago.'

'So I understand. But lots of boys lose their mothers, Master. I'd hope that if my boys lost me, they would be brought up not to bully their sisters.'

Nico demonstrated his independence by throwing his spoon across the room and then complaining that he wanted it back. Boudewijn returned it, whereupon Nico promptly threw it again.

'I'm not playing that game with you, young master!' Boudewijn told him.

We thanked Trijntje for her answers and left her to deal with Nico's attempts to impose his tyranny on their house.

CHAPTER TWELVE

'Two families left to interview, Boudewijn,' I said as we opened the gate to the house of Wim Pienaar.

'Yes, Master,' he agreed. 'Master, may I ask you a question?'

'Of course, Boudewijn.'

'Are we getting anywhere?'

What I should have said to him was that he might ask me any question he liked except that one. 'I need to sit quietly and think about that, Boudewijn. But I think it must be a bad idea to theorize before I have collected all the evidence.'

'Why, Master?'

'Well, suppose you have a big decision to make in your life, Boudewijn. Let me pose you a hypothetical question.'

'A what?'

'A hypothetical question. Let's play at pretending,' I explained.

'Pretending what?'

'Suppose I tell you that I will pay your passage to go to the East Indies. I'll give you the money you need to set up a household and employ some servants. You can become very rich in Batavia, Boudewijn. Would you want to go?'

'I don't know, Master. I hear it is very hot there.'

'Yes, but you'll have a grand house, and servants to fan you.'

'It sounds very nice.'

'So, on the evidence you have so far, you would be likely to give it favourable consideration?'

'Who wouldn't?' said Boudewijn, his eyes glazing over as if he had forgotten that I had said it was a hypothetical question.

'Ah, but now I tell you that over half the Europeans who go to live there die young from horrible tropical diseases.'

'Do they?'

'I don't know, Boudewijn. This is all hypothetical, remember? But let's pretend it is true; would you want to go now?'

'Of course not, Master. I don't want to die young.'

'There you are, you see. If you had made the decision without all the evidence, you might have made a bad one. That's why I need to ensure that I have it all before I try to find the murderer.'

'But you don't think it's Jaco Zwart?'

'I wish I could say so, but I need to ask him another question. I want to know why he didn't come running when Joost was shouting for help. If he was innocent, wouldn't he be the first one there? He was the nearest, after all. But if he was the killer, he might well ignore Joost. He would not want to return to the scene of his crime, especially if Wolf might still be alive.'

'Still be alive? I thought the surgeon said he died at once?'

'Yes, within a minute or two. But that was still long enough to say something. I just wonder if he told Joost who did it, but Joost isn't telling us because he wants to take his revenge himself?'

Boudewijn rubbed his chin in thought. 'But that only makes sense if the killer is Jaco, because he could have attacked anybody else over the last few days. The one person he can't attack is the one who is safely in custody.'

'Maybe Jaco is better off locked up, then.'

'He would be, if he wasn't waiting to be hanged, Master. I expect he doesn't feel quite so lucky to be in jail if he thinks about that.'

'I can't imagine that many men awaiting a hanging don't think about it a bit, Boudewijn.'

We came to the next gate up the road.

'So this is Trijntje's uncle's house?'

'That's right. Wim Pienaar and his wife, Eva. Trijntje's mother Sophie is Wim's sister.'

'And where does she live?'

'I don't know, Master. She never lived here, that's all I can tell you.'

'Do you mean that she did not live in this house, or in this village?'

Boudewijn appeared to be taxed by this simple question. After some moments during which his face contorted with the effort of explaining this conundrum to me, he launched into a response. 'The thing is, Master, that in a small place like this, sometimes we run out of women. I suppose at other times we run out of men too.'

'How do you mean, "run out of women", Boudewijn?'

'I mean that from time to time there are more men looking for wives than there are women looking for husbands, so we have to look further afield. That's one reason why so many of us go to Leiden on market days. We don't all have something to buy or sell, but there's never any shortage of young women in the city. I was lucky, because I found a local woman who knows our way of life, but, as you heard, Wolf had to go to Koudekerk to find a woman.'

'And how are things now, Boudewijn?'

'I fear for my brother Gillis,' he explained. 'There are only a few young women in Oegstgeest of marriageable age. There's the mayor's daughter, Joanna, of course, but the mayor won't allow her to marry the likes of us. He has his eyes set on some merchant or professional man, I'll warrant.'

I knew exactly which professional man was being lined up as a possible husband. The idea was not an unpleasant one, but on the other hand I relished having my freedom. I doubted whether a wife would be happy if I spent my evenings in Steen's inn, for example, which is where I like to do my work. However, it did not take much imagination to see that this was a serious concern for men of Gillis' age. It is sadly the case that women's lives are often cut short by the travails of childbirth, so many men will have two or three wives in their lifetimes, and since the Good Lord provides roughly equal numbers of boy and girl babies, there are periodic shortages of available women. If it were not for the fact that every so often we have a war to even up the numbers by killing off young men, who knows what mischief might result?

My eyes had been completely blind to this (as to so many things) but now that Boudewijn mentioned it, I recollected that on my walks through Oegstgeest over the past few days I had seen several young men but not many young women.

'What are you thinking, Master?' Boudewijn asked, interrupting my reverie.

'Nothing to the point. Let us go into the Pienaars' house and see what we can learn.'

The Pienaars were as hospitable as the others had been. Wim Pienaar was a jolly, burly man with a red nose caused not by drink but by the elements, and his wife Eva proved very willing to give her opinion on any topic I raised, and quite a few that I did not.

'I would stake my life that Jaco had nothing to do with it,' she stated boldly. 'He and our nephew Abraham have never exchanged a cross word.'

'How did Abraham come to be living next door?'

Eva was about to launch into an answer when Wim got in first.

'The tenant there died. I knew that Abraham was tired of working for someone else and had been looking for a place, so I put in a word.'

This was a complication that I had overlooked. 'Are you all tenants?'

'Aelter owns his, and I'm not sure about Smulders, because he was trying to buy his place outright, but all the rest of us rent, Master. We'd never raise the money to buy a holding as big as these.'

'So it's not certain that Joost Wolf will be able to take over the lease, even if he wants to?'

Eva's intense blue eyes were aimed directly at mine. 'I suppose not, Master. His uncle had only the lease. But what else would Joost do? It's all he knows. To think he'd lose his father and be put out of his home…'

'But look at it from the landlord's point of view,' Wim added. 'If Joost wants it and he can pay, why would he refuse? He'd only have to find a replacement, and there'd probably be a while when Joost had gone and the new man hadn't arrived and he'd get no rent at all.'

'Joost is hoping that some kind people might be willing to help him get a start,' I suggested tentatively.

Wim and Eva looked at each other before replying. Their silence spoke volumes.

'Well, I suppose a man's not to blame for what his father was like,' Wim conceded. 'And it would be a Christian thing to do, not that we could give much. But I'd give him a day of my labour to knock that place into shape, Master.'

'And if he needs any sewing or patching done, I can use a needle,' Eva added.

'That's very kind of you both. I'll pass it on,' I said. 'Tell me, did Wolf have any enemies?'

'Most of mankind, if you believed him,' Wim replied. 'He had a wonderful gift for falling out with people and blaming them.'

'Did you fall out with him?'

Wim seemed confused. 'Not through anything he did to me, but Abraham had arguments with him about that confounded pig.'

'The pig never troubled you?'

'He snuffled round once or twice, but when he saw me he'd slip away, Master. I've no idea why, but then who knows what goes through a beast's mind?'

I could imagine that where we saw a burly man with a loud voice, the pig had interpreted Wim as some large animal with a fierce roar and decided to seek his snacks elsewhere. 'But otherwise you didn't argue with him?'

'No, Master. We keep ourselves to ourselves here. And, remember, he was on the other side of the road.'

Wim said it as if crossing to the Hoeks' house opposite would be a major expedition, whereas a lusty youth could be there and back during the singing of a psalm.

'Did you know mevrouw Wolf?' I asked as nonchalantly as I could.

'Yes, we did,' Eva said. 'Such a sad woman.'

'Sad? In what way?'

'She had no life to speak of, Master. She wasn't from round these parts, but he brought her here and she tried hard to be a good wife to him. But after Joost was born we noticed she didn't talk to the rest of us so much, and I'd swear it was because her husband had told her not to. We saw less and less of her, and if we tried to strike up a conversation, on the way home from Divine Service, for example, he'd rush her off down the road, saying they had much to do that day and couldn't stand there yapping.'

I had heard of this. Of course, many would say that a husband is entitled to decide to whom he allows his wife to speak, though I cannot see how you can love someone and then seek to control their lives like that; but sometimes when a man is violent with his wife, we hear that the first step was to try to break her other friendships so that he had the whole of her attention. I was uncovering a consistent pattern of Wolf's behaviour, and I did not care for what I was finding.

'On the day that Wolf died,' I asked, 'did you see or hear anything?'

'No, Master,' Wim answered. 'Eva came to get me because Joost was shouting for help, though I admit I didn't hear him myself. Or, I suppose I ought to say that I heard a bit of a fuss somewhere but I didn't realise what was going on.'

'And did you go to him, mijnheer Pienaar?'

'We both did,' Pienaar replied, eyeing me as if to say that only a monster would not answer a neighbour's cry for help.

'And what did you see?'

'He was shouting that his father had been murdered, and I told Eva it was no place for a woman and to comfort the lad while we men took a look,' said Wim. 'When we got there mevrouw De Boer's boys were already there, and Lenaert wasn't far behind. Then I noticed that damned pig — begging your pardon, Master — that pig was strolling around in the road again, so I thought I should tether him up somewhere.'

'The pig was injured, I understand.'

'He was,' agreed Wim. 'There was a deal of blood on his flank, but he wasn't limping. So far as I could see, he was gashed on the side rather than on the leg. He wasn't badly pained with it, though it was quite a deep cut.'

'Do you have any idea how he came by such a wound?'

'Oh, that's simple, Master. Someone took a knife to him.'

'He couldn't have caught it on a nail, for example?'

'The edges weren't ragged enough, Master. No, it was a knife.'

'Wolf claimed that mijnheer Zwart attacked his pig with a knife.'

Pienaar shook his head. 'Why would anyone do that? It isn't in Jaco's nature to hurt an animal anyway. He's more likely to take a knife to the owner than to the brute.'

'Don't say that, Wim!' Eva scolded him. 'It makes it sound like we think he's guilty.'

'If he isn't, who is?' I asked. It was intended to be both silent and rhetorical, but I did not manage either. I have a bad habit of inadvertently voicing my thoughts, just as I did then.

'The thing is, Master,' said Wim, 'if you're looking for someone who didn't get on with Franciscus Wolf, you'll have nearly the whole village to consider, and that's a fact.'

'You can't argue with mijnheer Pienaar,' said Boudewijn as we trudged up the road to the last house on the left. 'It seems that nobody around here cared much for Wolf.'

'That may be true, Boudewijn,' I replied, 'but even an unpopular corpse is entitled to justice. If we're allowed to go around killing people just because we don't like them, what will become of us all?'

'There'd be a lot more of us walking around dead,' Boudewijn commented. I glanced at him to see if he was aware of the illogicality of what he had just said, but his face displayed a clear earnestness.

'Our Lord commanded us to do unto others as we would have them do unto us. We would want justice for ourselves, and therefore we must seek justice for Franciscus Wolf. If we depart from that principle, we become as savages, Boudewijn.'

'Have you ever had to investigate the death of someone you didn't like, Master?'

'Yes, Boudewijn, a man called Van Looy, and it taught me two things. First, the lesson I have just shared. I must try as hard to find the killer of a sinner as I would the killer of a saint; for upon arrival before God, the sinner who repents is just as assured of salvation.'

'And the second, Master?'

'The second was that I was wrong to dislike him, Boudewijn, quite wrong. He was a man playing a part, serving the Stadhouder faithfully, and artfully concealing his true self. And if I can be wrong about him, I do not doubt that I may be mistaken about any man.'

'We all can, Master. But can everyone be mistaken about the same man in the same way?'

'We were all deceived about Van Looy. Nobody had a good word to say about him.'

Boudewijn pondered over this as we walked up the road to the home of Claas van 't Bos and his wife.

Claas was a huge man, fair-haired, pink-skinned, probably around thirty years old. He was chopping wood in front of the house when we arrived, confidently allowing the axe to fall into the logs without a trial stroke. If I had done that, I would have passed my life without thumbs.

I introduced us and explained our purpose.

'Franciscus Wolf? Let me know when you find the man who killed him, Master. I'd like to shake his hand.'

'You do not mourn the death of another human being?'

Claas considered briefly. 'I am sorry for his boy. But as for the man himself, I bore him no love.'

'What did he do to you to give you so low an opinion of him?' I asked.

'To me? Little enough. His pig was a nuisance, but easily enough dealt with, and others suffered worse from that than I did. After all, he's a lazy brute and it's a fair walk to my land from Wolf's field, so he didn't come often. But the way Wolf spoke to women was not Christian, Master. I argued with him more than once about it.' He wiped his hands on a cloth, took a deep breath and continued. 'I may as well tell you, because if I don't others might. I had a long and loud argument with him less than a fortnight ago. It became fiery and I threatened him. But I didn't go through with my threats, Master. I swear I didn't.'

'What was the argument about?'

'My wife, Aagje, was walking back from the city after going to market. She was unaccompanied because I had work to do here, but an honest woman should not need a chaperone in public and in daylight. As she passed Wolf's house, he made a lewd remark to her. I'd rather not say what it was.'

'If it were lewd, then it is better left unsaid,' I agreed.

'When I saw she was crying I asked why and, she telling me the cause, I said that no man can allow his wife to be spoken to in such a way, and went down to talk to Wolf. He was unrepentant. He said if he spoke to her as a low woman, that was because she carried herself as a low woman.'

'And how did you reply?'

'With my fist. I knocked him clean off his feet.'

I could believe that. A punch from such a Samson could fell a donkey. 'And was that the end of the matter?'

'No, he picked himself up and ran at me, but I pushed him off. He and his son chased after me, but when I offered to fight either of them and told them only cowards would fight two against one, then the son slunk away and Wolf contented himself with using vile language and threats.'

'Threats?'

'That one day when I was away from home, he would show me what a whore my wife was. Master, at that moment I would gladly have killed him, but I give my oath that I did not.' He looked guiltily about him and lowered his voice. 'Please don't tell Aagje what Wolf said. She was mightily upset by the first speech and knows nothing of the second.'

'She won't hear of it from me,' I promised. 'But if you will fetch her, perhaps we could ask you both about your memories of the day Wolf died.'

Claas nodded mutely and went into the cottage to bring forth his wife. When she appeared, I could see that they were an odd match. Claas stood nearly a head taller than me, and when he stood a pace or so in front of me I could not see the cottage at all due to his broad shoulders, whereas Aagje appeared like a child's plaything, slender and less than the common height. Claas introduced us and told her that I had questions for them.

'Tell me, if you will, what you remember of the afternoon Wolf died.'

Aagje pointed across the road to the Smulders' cottage. 'It was Griet — mevrouw Smulders — who first told me of it. I heard Joost shouting something outside but I could make no sense of it, and it was she who interpreted his words.'

This surprised me somewhat, because Griet had claimed that she knew only what Gesina de Boer told her. 'Think carefully, mevrouw. Did Griet know this herself, or was she repeating what she had been told by another?'

Aagje thought a short while, then shook her head. 'I don't know. When I came to the gate, Griet and Gesina were talking — they're great gossips, Master — and then Griet came over to speak to me. Their men had gone to help, but I didn't see what Claas could do that Jan and Lenaert could not, so I did not go to him.'

This was interesting. If Aagje did not go to her husband, who could vouch for where he was at the time? 'Where was Claas?' I asked.

'Over beyond the small pond, I suppose. He was looking for something to bend into a screen or divider, hazel or willow or some such plant, so that we could build a shelter for the ducks.'

'You have ducks?'

Claas shook his head. 'They're wild ones, Master, but they come to the pond sometimes. I thought if they found the place well provided, they might settle here and give us extra meat once in a while.'

'And is that what you were about when Wolf was killed?'

'I think I must have been, for that's where I was that afternoon, though I didn't know Wolf was dead until Lenaert came to ask me to help draw the cart with Wolf's body on it. None of us has a horse of his own, you see.'

I had grown up believing that farmers lived lives of plenty, eating the fruits of their labours, enjoying good water and plentiful sunshine, free wood or peat to burn, and so on. It shocked me to realise that actually these families were poor. They survived, because they had something to eat, and they exchanged things amongst themselves to vary their diet, but I doubt that they had many guilders in ready money between them. The contrast with the citizens of the towns was stark. Even the life of the Mayor of Oegstgeest would have appeared luxurious to them, though in truth there were probably a hundred men in Leiden who lived as well.

A thought suddenly occurred to me. 'When did Joost accuse Jaco Zwart of the murder of his father?'

'As we were walking the cart to the church.'

'Not as soon as you gathered together?'

Claas shrugged. 'If he did, Master, then I didn't hear it. Yet Lenaert told me he had asked who had done it when he first saw Joost, for fear that there might be burglars in the area, and Joost had made no answer; but we put that down to the shock he was feeling. The boy was white and his wits were addled.'

'And when he finally accused Jaco, did he give any evidence?'

'He said that they had argued earlier, and pointed out that Jaco was the only man who played no part in attending to his father.'

'So he thought that Jaco might be guilty because he wasn't there?'

Claas lifted his hat to scratch his head as if this might stimulate his brain. 'I guess that might be so,' he said, 'but then I was only there to oblige Lenaert. If Lenaert had asked Jaco to draw the cart, I wouldn't have been there and maybe I'd have been the one who was accused.'

'But you didn't argue with Wolf on the same day.'

'Many men argue, Master,' said Claas, 'but they don't all go on to kill.'

CHAPTER THIRTEEN

The afternoon was growing dark as Boudewijn and I walked back to the town hall. The clouds were heavy with snow, purple and silver, and the sun made only a feeble effort to shine. On top of that, a biting wind was blowing up and I wished I had brought another fur-lined cloak with me.

'I'll warm some ale when we arrive, Master,' Boudewijn said, blowing into his cupped hands. It was only then that I noticed that he had no cloak at all, and felt guilty that I had been thinking of a second one.

'Before I meet your brother and his friend,' I said, 'tell me something of your life. How did you come to work at the town hall?'

'I didn't until the mayor was elected. That is, I worked for him in his business.'

'What is his business?'

'He sells things. Animals mainly, but also farms and estates. He holds regular sales and takes a commission on the selling price, and he's very good at getting men to compete against each other to push the price up. And he's known to be honest, so people are happy to trade with him.'

'Can't they make the sales themselves and save the commission?'

Boudewijn considered this concept and apparently found it to be revolutionary. 'I suppose they could, Master, but he arranges a lot of the sales beforehand. You don't have to wait for the market. He knows who wants a plough horse, for example, so when one becomes available he makes the deal quickly. You pay for his knowledge. And he guarantees payment. If anyone tried to welsh on a deal they'd made, he would let it be known and nobody would trade with them again.'

'So what did you do for him?'

'I still do it, Master. I draft his catalogues for his sales and get copies printed and put up around the villages and in Leiden. But he didn't need me every working day to do just that, so when he needed a clerk at the town hall he gave me that job. It saves him some of my wages, I suppose.'

'You told me you were married, Boudewijn.'

'Married two years, Master, to a fine girl.'

'A local woman, I think you said.'

'Yes, Master.'

'But your brother has not been as lucky.'

'I don't know as he's been properly looking, to tell the truth, but he bemoans the shortage of women here. He was a bit put out when mevrouw De Boer said she would go to Leiden with mevrouw Hoeks and didn't need him to carry for her, because he likes to go to Leiden to see if he can spy a likely catch. All honourable, I assure you, but when you work all day except part of the Lord's Day, that doesn't give you much time for wife-finding.'

Being celibate, I had never given the matter a moment's thought, and realised that I had only the dimmest idea how my father met my mother. I had always assumed that either you married someone who lived near you or you met someone at church or at market. My father went to church but he didn't linger after, and if he went to market he was working there. It now weighed upon me that since my grandmother's death I had nobody I could ask, so I would never know.

'May I ask, Master,' Boudewijn continued, 'if you're married?'

'No, Boudewijn.'

'No, I can't ask, or no, you're not married?'

'The latter. I'm not married.'

Boudewijn nodded. 'I suppose you don't get to meet women either, since there are none at the university.'

'There aren't any women students, but we have women to look after us. They do our laundry and prepare our meals.'

'But I expect it would be beneath you to marry one of them.'

'Nobody is beneath me, Boudewijn. We all have our place in life assigned by God, and what matters is not where that place is, but whether we measure up to it. You can be a good blacksmith and you can be a bad prince.'

Actually, I told myself, bad princes seem to be the norm. I exempted William of Orange from these strictures, who was a moral and upright man, just a little reckless when it came to his servants' necks; and his wife, the Princess Mary, was a pious and intelligent woman whom he had come to love deeply. Never mind that they looked like a heron and a pigeon when walking together.

'Forgive me, Master, I didn't mean to suggest…'

'There's nothing to forgive, Boudewijn. I took no offence.'

Boudewijn opened the town hall door and we walked inside. The mayor was not there and the fire had been allowed to die down, so Boudewijn's first job was to find some kindling and a flint.

'While you're doing that, I'll just have a few words with Jaco Zwart,' I said.

'As you wish, Master. The key is in the cupboard beside the mayor's work table.'

I pushed open the door to the mayor's office and found the small cupboard, removing the large iron key and carefully closing the cupboard behind me. I was mounting the stairs when it came to me that if the fire had gone out, that meant poor Jaco had been confined to a room in an unheated building for most of the day. The unfortunate man must have been nearly frozen by now, so I rushed to check that he was well. My fingers and thumbs refused to work properly as I hurried to turn the key, but eventually the lock clicked and I pushed the door back.

The room was empty.

I stood in some confusion in the doorway before advancing a couple of paces to see how he could have escaped. Suddenly I felt a blow on my back and heard the clanking of fetters as Jaco barged me aside and raced out through the open door.

A man with his ankles chained together is at a serious disadvantage when it comes to outpacing his pursuers, but so is a man wearing clerical attire, so it was no surprise that it was Boudewijn who managed to grab Jaco as he tried to open the front door with his manacled hands. Jaco swung round and hit Boudewijn with his arm, knocking the clerk to the floor, but the plucky young man was soon back on his feet and grabbed Jaco by the ankle chain as he tried to leave. The sudden brake caused him to pitch forward, and by the time I arrived Zwart was lying face down in the street with Boudewijn spread-eagled on his back. The passers-by stood transfixed as we returned the prisoner to his feet and forced him back inside and up the stairs.

'What were you thinking of?' I demanded. 'Surely you see that this makes you look guilty?'

Jaco was kneeling on the floor. He looked up at me, and his eyes filled with tears. 'Guilty or not, I am lost,' he whispered. 'I will never see my Sara again. I just wanted to see her, to embrace her…'

'I see no reason why she cannot come to you here.'

'I will not have her see me in chains. I will not expose her to the hostile stares of strangers.'

'She can come by night.'

'She will not leave the children.'

'She left them to find me.'

Jaco's chin dropped to his chest and his tears flowed freely. 'There is no hope, Master.'

'St Paul tells us in his Epistle to the Romans "we glory also in tribulations, knowing that tribulation worketh patience; and patience trial; and trial hope."'

Jaco raised his eyes to mine again. 'St Paul knew where his hope was coming from. But I have prayed night and day, and I'm still here. Am I forsaken?'

'We are never forsaken by God, Jaco. Never. But He works through human hands, and sometimes that takes longer than we would hope. I am doing all I can, as I promised your wife. Just answer one question for me — why did you not run to Joost's aid when he cried out for help?'

Jaco shook his head in confusion. 'I thought it to be a provocation. If I came out I would find him lying in wait for me, or his father likewise.'

'He was saying that his father was dead.'

'Aye, he said so; but when I left him just a couple of minutes earlier he was alive and well, so why should I pay any heed to such nonsense?'

'You did not come because you thought it was a trap?'

'Of course. Wouldn't you?'

Put like that, I suppose I would. If I had a heated argument with someone, walked away and a couple of minutes later I was told that he was dead, I think I would too.

I wrapped a blanket around his shoulders and gave him a manly clap on the back. 'Come, Jaco, don't distress yourself.'

'The farm will be going to ruin,' Jaco wailed.

I had no answer to this, but Boudewijn did.

'Jaco, there's precious little you can do there at this time of year and in this weather.'

Jaco admitted it was so by dropping his head onto his chest.

'I'm going to question some more people,' I told him. 'Please don't try to escape again. You won't get away, and everyone will know where to look for you. Try to be patient.'

As I left the room, I heard Boudewijn whispering to Jaco.

'You can trust the Master, Jaco. He's working really hard to find the killer, and I'm helping.'

I was unsure that this would give Jaco any additional comfort, but then I realised how uncharitable I was being, and silently prayed for forgiveness for it. On any fair assessment, Boudewijn was being helpful in introducing me and giving me local information.

As we warmed ourselves by the fire, the door opened and two young men entered, respectfully removing their caps as they did so. At least, the dark-haired one removed his, then plucked the other's cap off his head and shoved it into his hands.

'Master, Boudewijn said you wanted to talk to us.'

'So I did. Please, come by the fire and warm yourselves. Which of you is Gillis and which is Gerrit?'

The dark-haired one spoke again. 'I'm Gillis.'

My curiosity was piqued. If Boudewijn's mother had never known a man again, how did he come to have a brother?

'Can you begin by explaining your relationship to Boudewijn?'

'He is my half-brother. We have the same father, but different mothers.'

It was easy once you knew, like so many things. 'So you must be Gerrit Hoet,' I said, as much to cover my confusion as for any other reason.

'Yes, Master,' said the lad, who was clearly astonished by my feat of deduction.

These two were well-presented young men, Gerrit much the more muscular, but both of them well able to do a man's work. I suspected that Gerrit would need some supervision, because I doubted that his intellect was of the highest quality. He was not an idiot, you must understand; and it may be that if he had received better schooling, his future might have been different, but as it was, he was already destined for a life of hard labour of one kind or another.

'You know that mijnheer Wolf was killed the other day?' I began.

Both nodded.

'You were working for mevrouw De Boer at the time, I believe.'

'We were in the back field,' Gillis volunteered. 'The lady had us manuring the soil ready for ploughing and sowing when there is no danger of frost.'

'Manuring?' I said. 'Isn't that hard work when the ground is cold?'

'It is, Master, but it must be done at least three months before sowing root crops. That's why the lady was so insistent, because we were a bit late starting on it.'

Gerrit felt that he should say something. 'The soil isn't frozen yet, Master, so it can be done, but it's not pleasant work. And the mevrouw buys her manure now because it's cheaper than it will be in spring.'

I saw Gillis give Gerrit a nudge with his elbow, as if he might be speaking a little too freely about their employer.

'Where do you buy the manure?' I wondered.

'Mainly from dairy farmers outside the village, but mijnheer Wolf used to sell the pig's droppings too,' Gerrit told me.

'Really he needed them himself,' Gillis explained, 'because his own fields could do with manuring, but it was ready cash and Wolf always needed that.'

'What state is mijnheer Wolf's farm in?'

Gillis shook his head. 'It needs a lot of work, Master. The buildings are coming apart and he has no good water of his own. If he ever collected rain in a barrel it would help, but his fields are poorly kept and he just scythed the weeds instead of plucking them up.'

'But someone could make something of it if it were passed on?'

'They could,' Gillis admitted doubtfully, 'but what would you live on while you did it? Unless they have a store of grain or family to provide for them, it would be hard.'

'Joost is hoping he can take it over,' I said.

'Joost?' said Gerrit. 'Joost Wolf?'

'Yes.'

The boys looked at each other in confusion.

'He has less idea than his father had,' Gillis finally blurted out.

'He's hoping people will help him set up there.'

Gerrit scratched his head. 'Well, he's only one mouth now, and they may have turnips or beans in store, I suppose. And he could sell that pig. It's getting overmuch fat on it now. It needs to be worked harder to build up its muscle.'

'How do you work a pig? Aren't they lazy?'

'You scatter his food around so he has to walk about to get it. And that pig needs more greens.'

'You seem to know a lot about pigs, Gerrit.'

'My father has a couple, Master. But he also has four sons, so I have to earn my keep elsewhere.'

I had never given a moment's thought to the position of someone like Gerrit. Presumably at some point the farm would go to his elder brother; and even if his brother kept one or two brothers working for him, when he had sons of his own they would no longer be needed, by which time it would be late to make a new life for themselves. The trouble with farming in our country is that too many farms can only just support a family with a little to sell; and given that we are increasingly an urban people, living in cities with no land of our own, we buy food that the farmers can barely spare. As we had discovered a couple of times in the past ten years, we were at risk of famine if the crops were not good, or if an enemy invaded our farmland. In the hard times of 1672 we had been fed at the University, but only because the authorities confiscated food for essential people like soldiers and, surprisingly, us.

'Tell me, if you will,' I continued, 'what happened on the day that Franciscus Wolf died? What did you see or hear?'

Boudewijn passed round beakers of hot ale as they answered.

'It was an ordinary day until mevrouw De Boer returned from shopping in Leiden,' Gillis began. 'The ladies were coming up the road towards us…'

'How did you know that?' I asked.

'Mevrouw Hoeks' voice carries,' Gillis replied, while Gerrit smirked. I imagine that mevrouw Hoeks could make herself heard over quite a distance.

'We were working at the back,' Gerrit continued, 'but we can see quite a distance. If the ladies stayed in the middle of the road, we wouldn't be able to see because Wolf's house would be in the way, but mevrouw De Boer walks to the edge so she can see if we're working.'

Gillis gave Gerrit another nudge with his elbow.

'What?' snapped Gerrit irritably.

'Mevrouw De Boer is entitled to check on us, Gerrit,' Gillis explained to his friend. 'She pays us for a day's work, so she is within her rights to see that we're working.'

'And when did we ever do otherwise?' Gerrit rejoined. 'We earn our money, Gillis. We don't sit on our ar— I mean, begging your pardon, Master, on our bottoms doing nothing.'

'So,' I interrupted, hoping to stamp on the flames before the fire raged harder, 'you heard the women approaching. What then?'

'Joost was at the back of their house. We could see him feeding the pig,' Gerrit recounted. 'But then we heard shouting.'

'Who was doing the shouting?'

'Old man Wolf.'

'Could you hear what he said?'

'Not clearly. But it was something to do with that pig. Anyway, the women went past, and it became quiet again.'

'Just a moment. You said there was an argument. Did Jaco Zwart say anything that you heard?'

'He said something about Wolf being ridiculous.'

'And were their voices raised in anger?'

Gerrit looked perplexed so Gillis took over the testimony.

'Not at first. In fact, I don't think Zwart's ever was. But Wolf became louder after the mevrouw had come round to give us our orders.'

This was curious. It must have taken the two women some time to walk past Wolf and reach their own gates, and yet the argument had continued although, it seemed, only one party was interested in pursuing it.

'And what happened next?' I asked.

'Mevrouw De Boer was giving us a ticking off about something we hadn't done right, so I wasn't watching properly,' Gerrit explained, 'but then I noticed Joost move suddenly.'

'He moved? How?'

'I mean he got up from where he was sitting at the back of the house and ran round the far side.'

'And then?'

'Well, nothing really. I thought his father must have called him, though I didn't hear it. But then we heard Joost shouting for help.'

Gillis concurred. 'He'd run up to our gate and was shouting, then he carried on to the other gates. Like a mad thing, he was. So then we got out of him that he had found his father stabbed in front of the house. And by then mijnheer Hoeks had hold of him and charged him to tell us plainly whether his father was dead. And Joost said he didn't know, but he could do nothing for him, and begged us to run to him, which we did. I was the first one there.'

'And mijnheer Wolf was dead.'

'Yes, Master, but only just. The blood hadn't stopped flowing. I think that if Joost had been wiser and had stayed with him to tend to his wounds he might have survived, though we are a long way from any surgeon.'

'He might at least have told us what had befallen him,' agreed Gerrit, 'and he could have named Jaco as his killer, then your job would have been easier.'

There was no gainsaying that, though I doubt that Wolf died just to vex me.

It was growing late, so I thanked them for their assistance and let them go home.

'I'm off to Koudekerk tomorrow, Boudewijn, but I'll see you when I get back.'

Boudewijn's face portrayed his disappointment vividly. He had hoped to be coming with me, I think, but I had only asked to borrow one horse. 'I'll be here when you return, Master,' he replied. 'Have a good evening.'

The mayor's house was warm and inviting, and if I felt rather uncomfortable at imposing myself upon the household for a second time, they showed no signs of wearying of my company.

This time, Joanna was prepared for me. She wore a dress of a light brown shade with a white lace collar. Since she was indoors she did not wear a cap, but bore a circlet made of twisted wool on which small woollen flowers had been mounted. The whole effect was enchanting, though I confess that if she had stood before me in a hessian sack with a bucket on her head I might well have been just as smitten.

She took out her recorder and played a pretty little piece which, she told me, was entitled "What shall men do in the evening?" I have no idea what activity was portrayed there, except that presumably it kept them from rowdy behaviour in alehouses. I was acutely aware that the mayor was looking as much at me as he was at his daughter, gauging my reaction to her accomplishments.

'So, Master,' he said when the music concluded, 'you are off to Koudekerk in the morning. Are your enquiries bearing fruit?'

I did not like to admit that I could not see any progress, but equally I could not lie to him. 'There are suggestions,' I said ambiguously.

'Suggestions?'

'Matters that require elucidation.'

'Such as?'

I realised that I had dug something of a pit for myself, because the subject I wanted to discuss was not one for exposition in front of Joanna, where inappropriate suppositions might be made, but I had no choice. 'I need to find out why Wolf's wife Elisabeth chose to marry him, and why he chose her.'

'Forgive me, but how does that bear upon the case?'

'There are suggestions that he maltreated his wife and that her family may have taken revenge. However, they are not local people and no doubt they would have risked being seen and identified as outsiders.'

'Why did mijnheer Wolf marry a woman from Koudekerk?' Joanna blurted out, thus introducing the subject I was keenest not to speak about; and the mayor showed no sign of offering an answer.

'I understand,' I muttered, 'that there were insufficient young women in Oegstgeest to match the number of young men.'

Joanna blushed prettily. 'I suppose, then, that the girls' fathers chose the best men and those with less to offer had to look elsewhere,' she suggested.

'Indeed.'

'Father, surely the same is true now,' she announced. 'There must be two or three young men for every girl of my age.'

'And that is why we can anticipate a keen contest for your hand,' her father pronounced, 'and why we must be cautious in responding to their proposals. You only marry once, my girl, so we must make sure that your husband will care for you as you deserve.'

Joanna looked somewhat downcast.

'Never fear, child,' her father laughed. 'We will not marry you off against your will. But you must allow that your mother and I know rather more of life than you, and are better placed to judge the merits of young men.'

I began to feel very uncomfortable at the trajectory of this discussion, particularly the glances which each of them was directing my way, so I invented an excuse to get out of the way. 'Will you excuse me for a moment? I have left my handkerchief upstairs.'

As I left I realised that this was a ludicrously transparent excuse, since I had not gone upstairs since I arrived, but I was committed so I ran up to the bedroom to hide my confusion. I waited there a few moments to give them time to move on to a new subject, and was just about to return when I happened to glance out of the window.

A figure stood across the street gazing up at the upper floor. Since my room was in darkness I doubt that I could be clearly seen, but as the clouds shifted and the moon shone through I could see the upturned face of Joost Wolf. I did not know why he was looking at me like that, but it was a most uncomfortable feeling.

CHAPTER FOURTEEN

It was another wonderfully pleasant evening. To my delight mevrouw Gerrits steered the conversation round to my family, upon which I could speak without having to watch my words too closely. I told them of my father and mother, something of my late brother Laurentius, rarely far from my thoughts, and of course my dear grandmother, so recently departed then.

'So, sad to say, you are alone in the world, Master,' mevrouw Gerrits summed up.

'I am,' I admitted, 'though I have the constant company of my colleagues and students.'

This was hardly an unalloyed pleasure, and I fear they knew it, or at least Joanna's parents did. She simply gazed at me unnervingly. 'How exciting!' she said. 'I should love to be a student at the University.'

Her father laughed immoderately. 'You would be an adornment to them, I have no doubt, but whoever heard of a woman at a university?'

'You will forgive me,' I interrupted, 'but a learned lady of Utrecht, who has not long since died, was allowed to attend the lectures of the celebrated Voetius so long as she sat behind a screen or curtain.'

'Indeed?'

'Yes, her name was Anna Maria van Schurman. I have read her dissertation which asks whether women have the capacity for study and learning.'

'And what does she conclude, Master?' mevrouw Gerrits enquired.

'That a woman may indeed study well, mevrouw, as the lady proved. She spoke fourteen languages, I believe, as well as being an accomplished artist.'

'But did she marry well?' the mayor asked.

'I think she did not marry at all,' I answered.

'Well, then, how could she be said to have lived a happy life?' the mayor asked. Judging this to be the sort of question that admits of no satisfactory answer, or at least not one that would satisfy the questioner, I let the subject drop.

Since I had an early start in the morning, I was very happy when my hosts considerately suggested that I might need to retire, and in no time at all I was tucked into their spare bed, a much more comfortable specimen than my own bed at Leiden. Perhaps this explains why I very swiftly fell asleep, but early retiring also leads to early rising, and I woke before dawn.

For some reason, my brain was unusually active. On a normal day I stumble around and only really come alive when my breakfast is in front of me, but on this particular morning I was speedily alert.

I have come to realise what causes this. When I have a problem to solve, even if I have not clearly defined it to myself, my inner self continues to mull it over while the outer man sleeps; thus, while I had been in the land of slumber, my brain had worked out a way to solve this mystery.

The issue, as I saw it, was that all the witnesses were saying broadly the same thing, and together their testimonies made matters bleak for Jaco. In essence, he must be guilty because nobody else could be. But "broadly the same thing" is not the same as exactly the same thing, and a little voice told me I must write down what each witness had said before I forgot it, and then look for any inconsistencies or lacunae — gaps in the evidence, if you will.

I am blessed with an excellent memory, probably the result of having to learn things from books I could not afford to buy, so without any disputation with my inner self I climbed out of bed and found paper, ink and a nib in my pouch. I had not brought much ink, so I had to write with caution lest I run out before my hosts got up, but I set to and, I am proud to say, I was confident that within an hour I had captured their testimony on paper. At some point it would be good to go back and read it over to them so that they could make their mark on it as a true record, but for now I just wanted to read and re-read it to myself.

Having felt certain that this was the key to unravelling the mystery, it was chastening that when I had read it all over a couple of times I sensed myself to be no further forward. Perhaps, I wondered, I needed a more formal process of argumentation?

First question: what had Jaco and Wolf been arguing about in the first place? To which the answer seemed unequivocal. It was the depredations caused by Wolf's pig.

Second question: was Jaco's response disproportionate? It seemed not. Nobody claimed that they could hear his words in the argument, even when they could hear Wolf's.

Third question: Jaco left, apparently in control of his temper, then Wolf chased after him. Why did Wolf do so? Here the answer again seemed clear. He had observed some injury done to his pig — Wim Pienaar had vouched for the fact that there was such an injury, caused by a knife.

But here we had a gap, I suddenly realised. Mevrouw De Boer and mevrouw Hoeks had seen the men arguing in the lane. That much seemed incontestable. But Wolf was found inside his gate, so if Jaco stabbed him, he must have followed Wolf when that phase of the argument was over. Nobody had witnessed this, but it was the only explanation. Now we had another puzzle. If, as the women said, Wolf was aggressive but Jaco was calm, why had Jaco followed him? According to Joost it was so that Jaco could see the pig's wounds for himself. But why would he do that if he were the attacker? He would already know there was a wound. To give the impression of innocence, then? Well, perhaps.

At this point, there was a knock on my door.

'Master?' Joanna called.

'Yes?'

'I'll leave hot water outside your door.'

'Thank you.'

I rushed to open the door, hoping to catch a glimpse of her, but she was almost too quick for me. As I looked out she was just returning to her own room next to mine, and I caught a fleeting glimpse of a shapely pink ankle and bare foot as she turned in through the door. No artist ever captured anything more beautiful, and I was standing spellbound when her parents' door opened and I suddenly realised that I was not dressed properly myself. I quickly stepped back and closed the door before anyone saw me in my shirt, which would have been very unbecoming to a man in my station in life. It was then that I remembered that I had forgotten to pick up the pitcher of hot water, and carefully opened it again while I made myself as small as I could.

'Good morning, Master,' said the mayor. 'Is everything all right?'

I realised then how ridiculous I must have looked. 'Perfectly, thank you.' I said, rising to my feet. 'Your daughter was kind enough to bring me water.'

'Ah,' beamed the mayor. 'And very properly you were listening to check that she had returned to her room before opening the door. Such tenderness of feeling does you great credit, Master,' he continued. 'Breakfast will be ready in ten minutes or so. I'll just check they've brought your horse.'

Should I have corrected his misconstruction? Perhaps, but I let it pass, resolving instead to add it to the list of misdemeanours to be mentioned at my next Confession.

I shaved rapidly, given the coldness of the air, and donned my clothes, beating my robe softly with a book to shake off any loose dirt. In the chamber downstairs Joris Gerrits was warming his hands by the fire. It was a peat fire and therefore had been carefully banked the night before to ensure that it did not completely die down. Since they apparently had no maid, but only a cook, I assumed that this was something to which mevrouw Gerrits attended herself, in which event she would probably have passed on the skill to her daughter. This delighted me, because too many of our young women rely upon maids for tasks that they have not themselves been trained to perform. As a boy I watched my mother trim and gut animals for the pot, but I doubt that many young women of, shall we say, the better stations in life could have done the same. To my mind, this made juffrouw Gerrits an even more desirable catch, given that it was doubtful that any maid of any ability would consent to work for the kind of wages I could afford to pay.

I was, of course, getting ahead of myself. There was the considerable obstacle of my vows of obedience, poverty and celibacy to overcome. I had never had much problem with poverty, with which the University assisted to a considerable degree by paying me a pittance, nor with obedience, since my Bishop was a long way off in another country and rarely tried to communicate with me, but celibacy was another matter.

As a lecturer in a university which was, despite my protests to the mayor the night before, very much a male institution, I had passed much of my adult life away from the snares of women, but this role of investigator into which I had been involuntarily thrust pushed me out into the world and forced me to converse with females. It was becoming increasingly easy to understand how Eve had overcome Adam. An attractive woman can be very persuasive, and I was as certain as I could be that if Joanna Gerrits had suggested a lifetime of passion in exchange for the occasional black Mass I would at least have thought about it. I hope I would have refused, but you never know until it happens, do you?

The horse was tied up to a rail outside the house, perfectly content to stay there since his nose was plunged deeply into a nosebag. I do not impugn horses in general if I say that this particular specimen seemed not to realise that if he moved the bag would go with him, and chewed happily while tethered to a rail that he could have uprooted with the minimum of effort.

I loaded my travelling belongings in the saddle bag. Although I was to return the horse later, it might not be convenient to collect them, so the mayor gave me directions to the stable from which he had been hired. His name, it transpired, was Mercury, so we had something in common, though it was largely that we were both misnamed. Even the stable boy who brought him was not barefaced enough to claim that Mercury was fleet of foot, though I was assured that he would walk all day if I required it.

We set out for Koudekerk. On foot, it would take about two and three-quarter hours from Oegstgeest, I was told, but the horse should take about three-fifths of that time. Our route skirted Leiden to Leiderdorp, then we would follow the Oude Rijn. I was solemnly warned to follow the left bank, because if

I took the high road on the right bank I would have no easy way to cross over at Koudekerk.

Mercury plodded on in his sedate way, until I began to think that we would go faster if I got off and walked him, which defeated the purpose of hiring the brute, but then I noticed that the nosebag had been hooked on the saddle. Returning it to the animal's front end produced a marked improvement in temper and tempo, and in no time Mercury was moving at a gentle trot.

I could not help but notice that Mercury wanted to pull to the left, and in Leiderdorp it became clear why. We had to cross a small canal, which the stubborn animal was reluctant to do. It seemed that I had found one of the few horses in the world that did not like water.

After coaxing, threats and the use of some unclerical language, I induced him to cross by rolling an apple in front of us. Thus distracted, he consented to follow it and we came across the bridge and returned to our route.

To make my happiness complete, it began to rain, which soon turned to sleet. Mercury tried to turn his head, as if to ascertain whether I really intended to make him continue in such weather, but since we were in open country I had no choice but to press on, and when he saw the collection of cottages that constituted Koudekerk he resumed his trot in the hope of finding shelter there.

I had not thought to ask Elisabeth's family name, but given the small population I was hopeful that I would soon discover how to find her relatives, and so it proved.

'Yes, I knew Elisabeth,' one old woman told me. 'She married a man called Vos.'

'Wolf,' I corrected her. I suppose a fox and a wolf are easily confused.

'Ah, that's right, Wolf. Nice girl. But she's dead these many years, Master.'

'I know that, mevrouw. I am trying to find her family.'

The old woman pointed along a lane. 'You see that house where the lane bends?'

'The one on the right with two windows?'

'That's the one.'

'Thank you.'

'Well, that's not it. But if you look to your left as you pass it you'll see a yard, and that's where her brother works. He's a tanner. The mother lives with him. I don't know what befell his other sister, but he'll tell you.'

I spurred Mercury on, and in a couple of minutes we came towards the bend. Long before I could see the tanner's yard, I could smell it. It surprises me that tanners and others who ply noisome trades are allowed to set up close to people's houses, because the copious quantities of urine and dung they need are not pleasant to encounter.

I am not well informed on the tanning process and frankly I like to keep it that way, so I will content myself with observing that there were three large tanks, one containing fresh water, one containing urine and the third containing a solution of some other odoriferous muck. While I was there, villagers turned up with buckets of urine to deposit in the tank. It appeared that the buckets were tallied and after a certain number had been delivered a payment was made. Maybe I had spent too long chasing criminals, because my first thought was that where there is money there is theft, though who would try to make a living stealing buckets of ... well, never mind. It was just an idle thought.

If Mercury was wary of canal water you can well imagine how he felt about being tethered near those tanks, but I put his nosebag back on and he seemed mollified by this concession. Even if he was not hungry he could sniff the contents, I suppose.

A young fellow came forward to meet me. 'How can I help you, mijnheer?'

'I think I may be looking for your master. I have ridden here from Oegstgeest, where I believe his sister used to live.'

The boy looked doubtful but, following some cogitation with associated facial gurning to indicate the effort that was involved in that, he consented to fetch someone. After a little while a man approached. He was about Wolf's age, which would be right, and wore a long leather apron over a leather jerkin. I was pleased to see that he was wiping his hands on a rag as he approached.

'I hear you're asking about my sister, mijnheer.'

'Not directly about her, but I'm afraid it's all I know about you. I am Master Mercurius of the University of Leiden, and I am assisting the Mayor of Oegstgeest in investigating the death of one Franciscus Wolf, to whom I believe your sister was married.'

I do not suppose that the phrase *De mortuis nihil nisi bonum* has much currency in the mouths of tanners, because the sentiment was clearly unknown to this one.

'So the bastard is dead, eh? Proof that God answers our prayers, dominie. I hope it wasn't quick.'

'Actually it was. Somebody stabbed him to death.'

'And you're trying to find out who that was?'

'That's right.'

'When you find him, please let me know. I'd like to shake his hand and buy him a drink.'

'I understand your feelings, given the little I know of your sister's life, mijnheer...?' I fished for his name.

'Immers. Luuk Immers. Elisabeth was my sister.'

'And you have a brother, I believe?'

'Benjamin, my younger brother by eight years. But he has been taken from us.'

'My condolences,' I said automatically.

'No, he's not dead. He was taken into the Navy. He became a sailmaker.'

'Ah.'

'It's cleaner work, though there is more competition. But a sailmaker who can also work leather is at an advantage.'

'I see. And is he at sea now?'

'To be honest, I rarely hear from him. The last I heard he was in Amsterdam, where a fleet was being readied to sail to Curaçao.'

'He hasn't been anywhere near here, then?'

'Not since the Christmas before last.'

'And I am told your mother still lives.'

'Yes, by God's grace. She is past three score years and ten now, but she is still active. She lives with me in the cottage at the back there.'

'I see. Would you mind telling me when you were last in Oegstgeest?'

Immers pushed his cap to the back of his head to reveal his scowl. 'You think I might have killed him?'

'I do not make any accusation...' I stuttered.

'Look, Master, I'm as happy to take the credit as any man, but I haven't been to Oegstgeest for nearly six years. We all went when we heard Elisabeth was dead. He hadn't even sent word to us. Can you believe that?'

'So I have been told.'

'The minister of Oegstgeest came to find our minister, and that's how we heard. But by his account we knew she hadn't died a natural death. We're not rich, Master, but we asked a surgeon his opinion. Of course, she had been buried by then, but he asked questions of those who had seen her and told us it could have been caused by Wolf's treatment.'

'Why did he think that?'

Immers looked around to check that we were not being overheard. 'It seems that she told the other women there that she had a woman's complaint, but they told the surgeon it was not a normal woman's matter, but the result of damage caused within her by something he had done. And the surgeon said that the fever that took her could have been the result of the festering of such a wound, for the women who dressed the body said there was no outward mark on her. The surgeon had an interview with the mayor, but the mayor thought there was not enough proof to summon Wolf. After all, the surgeon had never seen Elisabeth.'

'You must have felt very aggrieved.'

'Aggrieved? If that's a fancy word for angry as a fox in a snare, then that's what I was. To lose a beloved sister was bad enough, but if it need not have happened, if it was caused by the act of her husband, that was extra pain.'

I felt instinctively that this man had nothing to do with Wolf's death, though I did not doubt him capable of it. 'How did they meet?' I asked.

'There isn't enough work in Koudekerk to keep me fully occupied, but Elisabeth and our mother used to go into Leiden to sell leather goods that they had made and to spread the word about our tanning business. They met up there. She used to look forward to market day so she could see him again.'

'Weren't there men here who were suitable suitors?'

'Certainly. Many of my friends would have courted her willingly, but Wolf was different, you see. He wasn't someone she had grown up with. Her head was turned, and that's all there is to it. Once a woman's made her mind up, you won't shift it. She was convinced Wolf was the man for her, and you couldn't talk her out of it.'

'You tried?'

'Mother tried mostly. Elisabeth wouldn't have paid any attention to me. She'd have said I was fighting my friends' corner.'

'And were you?'

Immers shrugged. 'There were some good lads there. Better than she chose, anyway.'

'Didn't your parents counsel her?'

'Our father was long since dead. Mother didn't believe she could change Elisabeth's mind. Besides, I think she took a shine to Wolf herself. She didn't do anything to stop them meeting at market. She was the only one who had met him before the wedding, when all is said and done.'

'You hadn't seen him?'

'He didn't want us to. Therefore she didn't want us to. He poisoned her mind against her own family, Master. It wasn't until she'd been married a while that she gave any thought to us, but she had no way of getting in touch.'

'Didn't she still go to market?'

'Not without him. Mother used to go with the leatherwork so Elisabeth knew where to find her, but if they did meet it was because Mother sought her out. And Wolf was always there too, so if Elisabeth had a mind to say something private she couldn't. But, to speak the truth, Master, I don't think she ever thought to say anything. To do that would be to admit she'd been wrong against my advice. Not that I cared one hoot about that.' His eyes glistened with tears. 'I'd have been happy to be proved wrong if it meant she was happy in her turn.'

I had learned all I could, I thought, and had no wish to observe such sadness. 'Thank you for your time,' I said.

'I hope you find whoever did this,' Immers said.

'I thought you wanted to shake his hand?'

'I do. But more importantly, I want everyone to know it wasn't me.'

'Is it convenient to speak to your mother?' I asked.

'Of course. You know where she is. She'll be pleased to see a minister of God.'

I picked my way across the yard, carefully inspecting where I was putting my feet, and with good cause.

The cottage door was open, so I tapped on it gently and entered. Mevrouw Immers was sitting by the stove slicing a fish into strips. I introduced myself.

'Come in, Master! Sit by the stove. I'll move.'

'No, please stay where you are. I'm well wrapped up. Shall I close the door?'

'If you please. I don't walk too well now. My grandson left it open.'

'You have a grandson? Was that the boy who greeted me?'

'That's right! That's Jan. But I have another, called Joost.'

I had overlooked the fact that Joost must be her grandson. 'I've met him,' I said. 'I've come here from Oegstgeest.'

She looked concerned. 'Is he all right?'

'He is fine,' I hastened to reassure her, 'but I'm afraid his father is dead.'

She looked down into the fire for a moment, then gave it a gentle stir with a poker. 'Dead? What did he die of?'

'I'm afraid he was stabbed.'

She nodded as she took the information in. 'It doesn't surprise me. He was a fiery type, that one.'

'I thought somebody should tell you.'

'Thank you, Master. It's a shame that nobody thought of that when my daughter died.'

I could think of no suitable reply, so I gave none.

'How is Joost faring?'

'I'm not sure,' I said. 'He plans to stay on and build the farm up again.'

She nodded again. 'I haven't seen him for five years or more. He must be grown now.'

'He's a strong lad. Physically strong. I'm not sure how he'll manage on his own.'

'He's not responsible for his father's actions, Master. Tell him he's welcome to come here if he wants. He won't want to live here, but he might like to pay a visit one day. I'll welcome him.'

'I'll tell him that, thank you.'

I could not erase the image of his face when he was looking up at me. Why was he so angry with me? Surely he understood that I was trying my hardest to find his father's killer?

CHAPTER FIFTEEN

Mercury and I were having a difference of opinion at the canal near Leiderdorp when I suddenly realised that I had omitted to ask an obvious question. What had happened to Jan's mother? I could not believe that it had any bearing on the matter in hand, but I was annoyed with myself for not noticing the absence of a woman of the right age in the house. I guessed that she too must be dead, because while Immers' mother could cope with the cooking, no Dutchwoman would have left the hearth in that state if they were able to do otherwise.

I decided to detour past the University to leave the contents of the saddlebag in my room, thus leaving me unencumbered for the walk back. While Mercury was still suspicious of water, he was distracted by the noise and bustle of the city and by the social opportunities afforded by the number of horses in view, consenting to be tied up at the back of the Academy where there were already a couple of other horses standing patiently while their carts were unloaded.

I emptied the saddlebag and climbed the stairs. In my joy at being once more on familiar territory, I had overlooked the fact that there was a certain window immediately above the place where Mercury was standing, with the result that I was intercepted at the top of the staircase.

'Ah, Master Mercurius!' beamed the Rector. 'I'm so happy that I had the good fortune to be here one of your occasional visits.'

It occurred to me that I had, perhaps, been taking his goodwill for granted and that I should probably have provided a fuller explanation for my absence.

'I realise, of course, that acts of charity are observed by Our Creator and stand to our credit in Heaven, but since it is unlikely that the University treasury will be going there, I wonder what exactly we are paying you for?'

Humility was called for. Fortunately, I am very good at being humble. 'I apologise profusely, Rector. I have not kept you informed as I ought. Nor did I acknowledge properly your help in examining the body of Franciscus Wolf.'

'Have you found his killer, Mercurius?'

'Not exactly.'

'This is a university, Mercurius. We deal in precision. The plausible answers are yes and no.'

'I'm a lecturer in the Faculty of Theology, Rector. "Not exactly" is common parlance there.'

Drelincourt smiled. 'Have you at least found the knife I described?'

'Not in the possession of the man charged with the crime. Or anywhere else, actually. But excluding the innocent is worthwhile, I'm sure you'll agree.'

'Of course. But I see you have a horse now.'

'Borrowed, Rector. I needed to go to Koudekerk this morning to interview some people there.'

'Suspects?'

'People who needed to be excluded. The brothers of the wife of the man who was murdered.'

Drelincourt turned this information over in his mind. 'Mercurius,' he asked, 'have you any idea what you're doing?'

'I am improvising furiously,' I admitted.

Drelincourt walked over to the window. 'You might offer that beast some water and food before he drops dead in our courtyard, and then come to my office. Perhaps over a glass of wine and some bread and cheese I can offer you an ear.'

The wine and cheese sounded very welcome. The accompanying inquisition did not. I returned to the courtyard and found someone who would take Mercury a pail of water and find him something to eat. I was concerned that there might not be anything suitable for a horse, but I need not have worried. Later in the afternoon, I spied Mechtild from the kitchen patting him on the shoulder and producing various tasty items from her apron. Her ministrations had always been welcome to me, especially after braving the charred victuals her husband Albrecht prepared. Nothing ever left Albrecht's kitchen underdone

Previous Rectors had always conducted their business with me across a desk or table, but Drelincourt preferred that we sit in chairs either side of the fireplace. A small table stood beside each chair, upon which I found a goblet of burgundy wine and a plate of bread and cheese when I returned. Drelincourt invited me to sit.

'You are very kind, Rector,' I said. There had been one Rector whom I had loved, who was excessively kind to me; the others tended for the most part to view me as a necessary penance inflicted upon them. However, they tolerated me for the very reason to which Drelincourt was about to refer.

'I am not unaware, Mercurius,' he began, negligently picking some imaginary lint from his breeches to avoid making eye contact, 'that your activities have brought some reflected renown to the University. And I am equally aware that you have no interest in fame or fortune.'

This was half true. Fame did not excite me, at least not for that activity, because I had learned that fame brought new commissions from people whose work could not be refused, such as our beloved Stadhouder. On the other hand, the gold he had given me on successful completion of my tasks was very welcome; not, you understand, because I am avaricious, but because it gave me the freedom to leave if ever I found Leiden uncongenial. [Marginal note: I never did, so I still have much of the gold, but it buys me a warm robe or a few books now and again.]

'But you must realise,' he continued, 'that your success brings expectation, and therefore failure brings disappointment, and disappointment will reflect badly upon the University. And that is why we must not let you fail.'

I found this strangely heartening. 'I am grateful for your support and understanding,' I stammered. 'I don't know quite what to say.' An unmanly tear was forming in the corner of my eye, which I flicked away with a finger.

'We are a collegium devoted to the pursuit of the truth, Mercurius, and in your own way you are contributing to the discovery of truth. Therefore, unlike some, I see your labours as a type of philosophical enquiry; not demeaning your position, but rather enhancing it.'

I was keen at this point to enquire who these "some" were who disparaged my efforts, but it seemed inappropriate to pursue that particular hare at that moment.

'So, come, man,' he said, 'and share what you know, and let us see if we can untangle whatever you have stored in that curious brain of yours.'

It would be tedious to the reader if I recount here once more the thoughts that had pressed upon me over the previous few days, so I will not do so. If you have forgotten anything, read the book again.

Drelincourt listened patiently, cradling his goblet and sipping at intervals. I will admit that he refilled mine, with the result that I drank rather more than I intended; and since I was talking, I did not eat much bread, and was therefore drinking on a largely empty stomach. And it was particularly good wine.

'It seems to me, Master,' he declared when I had finished my tale, 'that the problem here is that you have an ineluctable outcome, but you don't like it. Is there a risk that you are refusing to accept the plain truth because the plain truth is unpalatable?'

'No!' I said vehemently, by which I really meant yes, because I had already come to that conclusion myself. If I could not clear Jaco's name, he would go to the gallows and I would feel that I had let Sara down, not to mention his children. To me it seemed that a direct appeal from his wife would have gone unanswered. I grant that she was not paying for my services, but I would have felt that she had overpaid given the outcome.

'Explain to me, then, what reason you have for denying the obvious conclusion of your enquiries.'

It was not said unkindly. Indeed, in my student days several lecturers spoke to me much more severely than this, but I felt like a particularly obtuse specimen of studenthood at the feet of a kindly professor.

'I can't express it,' I said. 'It's a sense of incongruity. Something doesn't fit, but I can't think what.'

'In what sense?' Drelincourt pressed me.

'Well, it seems to me that logically a murderer needs three things. He needs a motive to commit murder, because most men do not kill to no purpose. He needs to have the means to do so. And both of these would be useless if the opportunity to commit the crime does not present itself. For example, there may be many men who would willingly kill the Stadhouder, but we protect him by making it difficult for armed men to approach him. We cannot do anything about their motives, but we can remove the means from them and we can deny them the opportunity.'

'So much seems logical to me. Pray continue,' the Rector replied.

'In this case, there seem to have been many people who might have had a motive to kill Wolf. Or, perhaps I should say that if dislike is an allowable motive, a great many people had an equal motive, because he seems to have made himself very unpopular. Many people freely admit that they would willingly have killed him. I have even had men tell me that they want to shake the killer's hand and congratulate him.'

'How sad!' remarked the Rector. 'I should hate to think that anyone will rejoice when I am gone.'

I had not thought of that, but I have contemplated it with increasing personal interest as the years pass. Will anyone mourn me? [My clerk Van der Meer says he will, which may be true, if only out of self-interest, since he will have to find another job.]

'As to means,' I continued, 'Wolf was killed with a long knife, as you know. I have not found a knife quite like it, but most of the farmers have a range of knives so I doubt that it is quite as distinctive a weapon as it would be here in the city. But the real problem I have is that while many have the means and the motive, only Zwart appears to have had the opportunity.'

'And yet you persist in thinking him innocent?'

I had to confess the illogicality of my position. Whatever I thought of him, I could not prove him innocent. I could, perhaps, argue that a man ought not to hang without some certainty of his guilt, and there was insufficient positive proof of that to warrant putting a noose around his neck, but I doubted that the judges would be moved by such a suggestion. Trials at the assizes are notoriously brief. The accused invariably protests his innocence (because if he had confessed, the local authorities would have hanged him without waiting for the judges), but a large proportion of trials end in a capital sentence. There are even those who tell you that an innocent man who hangs is fortunate, because he will automatically be admitted to Paradise due to his unearned suffering. I am not sure that this suggestion is as much of a consolation to the man choking on a rope as its proponents claim.

'If,' I began cautiously, 'I could be convinced that I had not overlooked anything, I would have to accept the probability of his guilt, Rector. But how terrible would it be if I failed to save him and only then thought of some important matter I might have raised, some argument I might have made, some clue I should have pursued!'

I took another large draught of wine to steady my emotions.

The Rector was carefully picking that invisible lint from his clothes again. This meant that his eyes did not look into mine and therefore his words seemed less aggressive. 'Consider, Mercurius, that you believe that no other had the opportunity because everyone is telling you so; but the real murderer must be among them, and he has every reason to mislead you.'

'One of them is lying to me?' I gasped.

'Incredible as it may seem, if this man Zwart is innocent, then such must be the case.'

'But they corroborate each other.'

'I'm sure they do. It would be a poor liar who did not harness the collective force of the opinions of others. The killer will tell you what you have already heard. But the means, from what you tell me, are always readily to hand; the motive is a long-held grievance of some kind, not a sudden impulse; and if the killer has planned this for some time, he may have engineered the opportunity after some degree of preparation, in which he will have concealed his own chance to kill.'

My brain was swimming. *If all this should be true, where do I go now?*

Returning to the courtyard with the Rector's blessing, I had to persuade Mercury that his lunch was over. Whoever had fed him had ensured the beast did not go hungry. I may have remarked before that my late grandfather was a blacksmith. I had no interest in or aptitude for such a trade, but I helped him occasionally as a boy, and while I know very little about horses I know that when you are shoeing the rear hooves you do not stand under the tail, which is wont to become a hazardous place at little or no notice. Judging by the activity beneath Mercury's tail, he had dined well.

I attempted to mount him, but I was impeded by the wobbliness of the stirrups. Wherever I moved my feet, the stirrups seemed to slip away from them.

'Are you all right, Master?' asked one of the yard lads.

'The stirrups,' I said, 'appear uncooperative.'

The boy stepped forward and took each of my feet in turn, guiding them into place. It seemed very much easier done that way.

'Thank you,' I said. 'Onward, Mercury!' Although I made encouraging motions with my knees and patted him on the neck, we seemed to make no progress.

'Perhaps if I untie him, Master...' the impudent boy suggested.

'Yes, yes, of course,' I snapped, feeling deeply embarrassed that this had not occurred to me.

I heard the Rector's voice behind me.

'Mercurius, I think perhaps you would benefit from lying down for a while. You seem a little … overtired. The lad can return the horse if you give him directions.'

'Yes, perhaps I am rather tired,' I admitted, and tried to dismount, but now the wretched stirrups adhered to my feet and the boy had to detach them for me. I swung my leg over the animal and unaccountably found myself lying on the ground.

'Horse must have moved,' I muttered as I was helped to my feet.

'Where shall I take him, Master?'

'Ah — I'm not quite sure. But if you go to the town hall and ask the clerk whose name is … well, whatever his name is, he'll direct you to the stables.'

I patted the boy on the head, thanked the Rector and climbed the stairs to my room; and he must have been right, because in no time at all I was sound asleep. It might have been better if I had made it to the bed, but the floor seemed quite comfortable at the time.

CHAPTER SIXTEEN

When I woke it was already dark, but I could hear the familiar sounds of the refectory: bubbling conversation, the clanking of tankards and platters, and the sound of doors swinging shut as men decided to eat elsewhere once they had viewed what Albrecht had prepared.

I must have wrapped my bedclothes around me somehow, for they were tangled about my shoulders. When I stood up, my head ached and my robe was severely creased. The embroidery of my counterpane had become embossed in my cheek so that my face appeared to have been branded with a fleur-de-lys. My mouth felt as if someone had shovelled sawdust into it, and I found myself strangely uninterested in food — even before I entered the refectory.

I collected a tankard of ale and took it out into the fresh air. This was, strictly speaking, an infringement of a regulation which did not permit drinking in front of the Academy building, but at that moment I cared little for any rule or by-law. There is a group of Dutchmen who believe that laws are useful to guide the conduct of others, but not themselves, and while I normally find that an unconvincing doctrine, at that moment I just wanted something to drink, nothing to eat, and clean air to breathe.

There was a rustle behind me as I sat on the steps. Turning to investigate, I found myself looking into the round and concerned face of Mechtild.

'Not joining us tonight, Master?'

'I fear something I had earlier did not agree with me,' I replied.

'That'll be why the boy took your horse back, then.'

'Yes. I must thank him.'

'Can I bring you something?'

'Thank you, but I don't think I could eat anything.'

'You didn't eat at lunchtime, did you?' she scolded me, and I could see by her frown that she knew why I had a headache.

'Some bread and cheese.'

'Yes, but precious little of it. What you need, young man, is something light and easily digestible to put some ballast in your stomach,' she told me sternly, and turned on her heel, returning in a moment with a clean cloth in her hands.

'Here!' she said, handing the bundle to me. It seemed ungrateful not to at least look at it, so I gingerly peeled back the cloth to reveal two perfect little egg custards.

'One now, and one later,' she instructed. 'Take it slowly, but there's nothing there to disturb the feeblest innards.'

'I thought pastry was bad for an inflamed stomach,' I protested. The glower on her face told me I had said the wrong thing.

'Pastry, yes,' she said. 'But not my pastry.'

I smiled feebly and broke off a portion. Since Mechtild was clearly planning to stand there until I had eaten one of the tarts, I put the piece in my mouth and slowly chewed. I could taste velvety egg and the sharp kick of nutmeg as the pastry crumbled and dissolved on my tongue. Finding that I had no urge to vomit after the first mouthful, I tried another and so, by degrees, I finished it off.

'That's better,' she said. 'You'll be glad of that later. Now, set the ale aside and I'll bring you a herbal draught.'

'What's in it?' I asked.

'Never you mind. It's a recipe passed down from my grandmother and doubtless from her mother to her, and entirely wholesome. A beaker of that and you'll be feeling brighter in no time.'

She returned after ten minutes or so with a horn beaker containing a hot drink. A couple of leaves poked out and I made a mental note to take a walk round the celebrated Botanical Garden in the morning to see which plants were missing foliage.

It was sharp tasting but oddly soothing. The bitterness made my tongue curl at the edges, so I closed my eyes and poured the whole lot down in one gulp. As I returned the beaker to Mechtild, she looked uncommonly satisfied.

'There's my brave soldier!' she said, before bending close to my ear and whispering to me. 'If you find your pee turns bright green, don't worry,' she said, and waddled off to her kitchen while I wondered whether I had just acquiesced in my own poisoning.

In vino veritas, they say, which is to argue that there is truth in wine. All I could detect in wine was a headache that was still lingering as I tried to deal with the business that had accumulated while I had been about my enquiries. One of my students had left me a note which strongly suggested that the last four months' teaching had been completely in vain so far as he was concerned. It depressed me to think that there might be others among the undergraduates who persisted in thinking that Abelard and Héloïse were a pair of philosophers and theologians, rather than a theologian and his girlfriend. The only feature of Abelard's life which seemed to have lodged in the student's brain was that he was castrated by a gang hired by Héloïse's uncle Fulbert. I can understand that for young men this is a noteworthy occurrence, and probably even more so for Abelard himself, but I had hoped that they had at least remembered the key points of Abelard's *Theologia Summi Boni* that I had spent some hours expounding for their benefit.

The head of the faculty wanted to know if I would be able to deliver the planned lecture series on Tuesday mornings, so I assured him that this was not in doubt. I would ensure that I was not in Oegstgeest even if I had not yet solved the murder. The truth of the matter was that I began to doubt the murder would be solved even by the end of the lecture series; except that, I suppose, Jaco Zwart would have been convicted and executed by then if I could not prove another's guilt.

Mechtild was right. The urine in my chamberpot was a vibrant shade of green. I am sufficiently fastidious not to empty my pot from my chamber window, not only because anyone standing underneath may not like it, but also because I think a civilised community such as a university should set higher standards, so I normally empty it in the runnel that leads to the canal. I do not feel comfortable asking the college servants to do it, so I covered it with a drape and descended by the back stairs. As I stepped outside the cold air made me feel quite light-headed, and I had to sit for a moment on a window-ledge until the feeling passed.

It is alleged that Martin Luther had some of his finest insights into his theology while sitting in the privy, so it is not altogether surprising that as I sat on the windowsill with my chamberpot on my knee a strange conviction came over me that I had been approaching the killing in Oegstgeest from quite the wrong direction. The difficulty was that I could not think what other direction I could take.

I rose unsteadily and made my way over the cobbles to the runnel, where I emptied my pot, having first looked about me to ensure that nobody was in view. It is not that there is anything inherently shameful in using a chamberpot — I am fairly sure that Our Lord himself must have produced human wastes at some point during his thirty years as a man — but that I did not want to be seen disposing of the contents so long as their colour might draw remark. It was entirely possible that someone might take this as a sign of witchcraft or some similar stupid superstition. Plenty of people had been burned alive at the Roermond witch trials on flimsier evidence than that.

I walked wearily back into the building, acknowledging to myself that I could not put off returning to Oegstgeest indefinitely. I would have to admit that my trip to Koudekerk had been fruitless and that I had wasted an entire day — a day and a half if you included my recovery time that morning.

On top of that, I would need to set aside some time to review my lectures on the apophatic way of perceiving God. I had given these each year for some time, so I doubted that they needed much work; and, in the way of such subjects, nobody with any real talent for theology appeared to have worked on the topic for a hundred years or more, so I doubted that I would find anything new that needed to be said.

Anyone observing me would have found my antics rather unusual that morning. First, I slunk secretly out of the building with a large object wrapped in a cloth in my arms, pausing to sit on a windowsill for a while before emptying the contents in a drainage channel. Next, I stood for some time in contemplation before, probably with bowed shoulders, I trudged back into the building. Finally, as I mounted the third stair, I stood with my foot hovering in mid-air before pirouetting on the spot and descending back to the ground. I have no doubt I looked something of a dolt standing there with my mouth open, but I can assure you, gentle reader, that my brain was working furiously as I began to shape an idea.

To explain this, I need to describe what apophatic theology is. I imagine that most readers will find this as exciting as the majority of my undergraduates and will sit there scratching their private parts or trying to touch the tip of their noses with their tongues, but I regret that it is necessary. I will not, however, give the full six hours of detailed explanation that constitute my series of lectures.

The idea behind apophatic theology is that while it is very difficult to say what God is, because we have not yet met Him, nor is human language adequate for that task, we may be able to describe Him by saying what He is not; thus, He is not mortal, He is not bounded by time or space, He is not Spanish (whatever our former masters may try to tell you). This way of negation may appear not to be constructive, but in fact if the attributes are skilfully chosen a useful description may be arrived at. I demonstrate this to students by placing an apple behind a screen and asking one student to describe what it is not while the others try to work out what he is looking at. All too often the attention span of the student fails and he eats the apple, thus negating the point of the demonstration of negation, but that is not important now. What matters is that I was forming the idea, somewhat inchoate at present, that perhaps I could learn something about the killing by what had not happened.

One of the advantages of walking everywhere is that I have plenty of time to think. Sometimes my thoughts are not particularly holy or philosophical, such as those occasions when I wish I had a horse, but on others I am able to do some deep thinking as I march along. So it was on the day of which I am writing; I was so wrapped up in my thoughts that I completely forgot to bear right on leaving the city and found myself almost at Castle Endegeest before realising I was walking to the wrong village. I veered to the right and picked up the path through the woods that led back to Oegstgeest, entering the village at the top of the lane that led past the fatal scene. The main part of Oegstgeest was before me, and people were bustling back and forth across the road.

Where was I to go first? Somehow I realised that I had not completely thought through my mental processes, and I decided that I must go somewhere where I might think without interruption. To be honest, I could have gone almost anywhere in Oegstgeest, because comparatively few people were interested in talking to an outsider anyway, but I did what I would have done in Leiden in such circumstances. I went to the inn.

The great advantages of an inn for a scholar are obvious. Almost nobody can read well enough to look at your book over your shoulder. So long as you are buying food and drink, you can sit there undisturbed, assuming that no itinerant lute-players offer to play for you in exchange for a drink. I have explained before that lute-players are one of the great hazards of tavern life, not to mention being men of the lowest moral standing and a threat to virtuous womanhood everywhere. Fortunately, there was no lutenist in Oegstgeest at that time.

I asked for a flask of small beer and sat as close to the fire as I could without falling into company with anyone else. My clerical garb spared me some conversation, because generally a minister in a tavern is bad for business, since men decide they ought not to get drunk in my presence, and the best way to avoid that eventuality is to pretend that you have not seen me. I was therefore assiduously ignored by the men there, until one was so oblivious to my presence that he tripped over my feet and ended up in my lap.

'Begging your pardon, dominie,' he stammered as I raised him to his feet. He was a young man of around eighteen to twenty years, appalled to think that he might just have involuntarily assaulted a man of God, thus showing that he had at least been brought up with good principles. In his fall he had overturned his beaker, and my shoulder was covered in beer which the innkeeper rushed to sponge off, presumably in case I placed the inn under an interdict or excommunicated all present.

'Not to worry, mijnheer…?' I said.

'Plattevoet. Daniel Plattevoet. I am mortified, dominie. Let me…' He took the innkeeper's cloth and rubbed so vigorously at my shoulder that my arm began to feel numb.

'It will clean later,' I told him. 'Please, sit here a moment and let me refill your beaker from my flask.'

He could hardly refuse, and the innkeeper was very happy to leave us alone now that he knew I was not going to summon St Michael and his angels to purify the place with fire.

Young Plattevoet would not sit on the bench beside me, but found a low stool on which he perched. The effect was rather like a bull attempting to imitate a frog, but he seemed comfortable enough.

'Mijnheer Plattevoet, may I ask how old you are?'

'Eighteen, dominie, so far as I know.'

'I am Master Mercurius of the University of Leiden, here to assist the mayor in discovering the murderer of Franciscus Wolf.'

Plattevoet's eyes opened wide. 'It wasn't me, Master!' he gasped.

'Nobody has suggested it was, mijnheer. But it would help me considerably if you could tell me something about Oegstgeest and its inhabitants.'

'What do you want to know?' he asked suspiciously.

'Well, Franciscus Wolf has a son, Joost,' I began. 'Do you know him?'

'Everyone knows Joost Wolf,' Plattevoet replied, his tone strongly suggesting that just because he knew him did not mean he was well disposed towards him.

'How would you describe Joost?'

'He's all right. A bit given to bragging, something of a dreamer. He has plans to leave here and make his way in the city.'

'Really?' To my recollection, Joost had said he wanted to keep the farm running.

'He says the life of a farmer's son isn't for him. He can't see himself doing it all his life. But I suppose now he has no choice.'

'He could sell his lease, I suppose,' I suggested.

'He could,' Plattevoet conceded, 'but there are better farms up for sale. I guess his best bet is to build it up over the next couple of years and then try to sell it.'

'That's what I think he hopes to do. He is optimistic that people here will help him to get it into better shape and maybe offer him some gifts so that he can improve it.'

Plattevoet nodded a couple of times. 'Well, Master, his father wouldn't have got a bent stuiver out of any man here, but Joost isn't a bad lad. People might feel more generous towards him, not that money is abundant in these parts.'

'There is a lot to do there, it's true. And it hasn't been helped by the loss of his mother,' I mused aloud.

'She was a nice woman.' Plattevoet smiled as he recalled her.

'You knew her?'

'Of course, Master. A little woman from somewhere beyond Leiden. We'd see her at church when we were young. If you played with Joost she'd always have a kindly word with you. Living out of the way where he did, he didn't have any close friends, so the only people he met were us boys at the school or the people at church.'

It had not struck me that a five minute walk down the lane meant that the Wolfs were separated from the bulk of village life. 'But Franciscus Wolf drank here, I assume?' I asked.

'Certainly, Master, and so did Joost once he was grown, not that he was a big drinker. He'd come in and talk a bit, then bid us a good night and head off home again. I think he was a bit lonely. He'd walk in with his father, but he wouldn't stay long before he walked home again.'

Plattevoet was painting a melancholy picture, to be sure. I had not stopped to think that poor Joost would now be lonelier than ever.

'Does Joost have a girlfriend?' I enquired.

'I wouldn't know, but I'd be surprised. There are very few girls in the village at present. Most of us can only meet girls at the market in Leiden.'

'Is that where you find wives?' I asked.

Plattevoet gave me a look that suggested that he had penetrated my Reformed exterior and somehow discovered that I was a secret Catholic priest committed to perpetual celibacy, who therefore should not be asking about how a man could snare a wife.

'I don't know how else you'd find one,' he mumbled. 'Of course, my father asks around now and again and our mothers are always on the lookout for a likely girl, but they're not easy to find.'

'Poor Joost has neither a father nor mother to help him,' I said. 'How will he find a wife, do you think?'

'He'll have some money, I suppose. And he won't have to ask his father's permission to go to market whenever he wants. It might even be easier. After all, a girl won't have to worry about how she'll get on with his mother, will she?' He smiled briefly, then looked downcast as he realised that his comment might be thought wounding to the memory of Joost's mother. 'I didn't mean … not that any girl would have found Joost's ma difficult to get along with.'

'I didn't take it that way,' I said. 'I know what you meant. I'm alone in the world now, but when my grandmother was alive if I'd so much as mentioned a girl she'd have rushed to check she was a suitable match for me.'

I had never actually had a girlfriend in that sense, so this was supposition on my part, though in recent years my grandmother had questioned me every time she saw me on my marriage plans, reminding me that while I was a remarkable catch for any woman of sense, I was above the age at which most men marry. She understood that my studies had to come first and someone had planted the idea in her head, of which I did not disabuse her, that any lecturer who married had to resign his post, as is the case in some universities. That was not the rule in Leiden, though the authorities generally preferred us to have no more than one wife at a time, ideally our own.

I thanked mijnheer Plattevoet for his information, assured him once again that the spillage on my robe was of no importance, and ventured out into the road where large flakes of snow were once more tumbling from the heavens. Needless to say, I had not brought a heavy cloak.

CHAPTER SEVENTEEN

Boudewijn greeted me like a long-lost brother returning from the East Indies. 'How is our enquiry going, Master?' he asked.

This is a curious feature of speech. I notice that whenever someone assists me in an investigation, it becomes "our enquiry", until such time as it begins to go wrong, when it becomes "your enquiry" again. I suppose the fact that Boudewijn was still prepared to accept some of the credit implied that he felt that we were making progress.

I explained what had transpired at Koudekerk, namely, nothing of importance to the matter in hand, and how I had detoured into Leiden on the return journey. I glossed over the circumstances that led to someone else bringing the horse back.

'The stable lad said you were unwell, Master. I hope all is now mended,' Boudewijn said.

'Thank you, I feel much better,' I said. Actually I did not, but when people ask "How are you?" they rarely want an accurate answer. Even my physician has to be reminded that if I were well I wouldn't be calling on him, so it may be worth his while listening to my answer to his question. 'They seem to be an unlucky family, Boudewijn.'

'Who do, Master?'

'Elisabeth Wolf's kin. Her brother had a young boy with him, but there was no sign of a mother, and Elisabeth's own mother was keeping the house.'

'A woman's life is ever fragile, Master. So many die young.'

'I suppose you're right. But he is a good man with a prosperous — if unpleasant — trade. You'd think he would be able to find another wife.'

'Perhaps his love is entirely with the first, Master.'

This is a conundrum I have never managed to unpick. I have known many a man over my lifetime who was utterly devoted to his wife, and she to him. Yet when one of them dies, the other remarries within a twelvemonth. I can understand that a man needs someone to keep house, perhaps to help bring up his children, and that a woman who has no husband is at a great disadvantage in this world unless she be very rich, in which event her chief concern is to fight off suitors, but it leaves me puzzled. How much are marriages founded on love, and how far on strictly practical concerns of security?

There was at one time — I digress, but no matter — a whore who plied her trade in front of the University. Her name was Fat Lysbeth. At least, that is what people called her. I doubt that she received that name at the baptismal font. She was a woman of some spark, tolerated in Steen's Inn because she never solicited customers there and was a good-natured person, generous and kindly in her own way.

I have no idea what impelled her towards a life of vice. In general, these women have suffered some great misfortune and their poverty rather than any desire to sin is their motive, and it may be so with Fat Lysbeth. I never asked, and she did not volunteer it. I mention her because once in Steen's Inn a man was disparaging about her mode of life to her face. He accused her of debauchery, depravity and various other long words, but unfortunately he included the word dishonesty in his catalogue. She took exception to this, and told him roundly that she was no more or less dishonest than any woman.

'I sell myself for money, that's true,' she told him. 'And I use that money for the necessities of life and a few comforts beside. But then your wife, mijnheer, trades her body for the comforts and security of your home. The deal is that she lies with you, and you keep her fed and clothed. I don't see that there's any great difference between us.'

'How dare you!' the man raged. 'There is a very great difference between you and my wife.'

'So there is,' Fat Lysbeth replied. 'I forgot. I probably enjoy my work much more than she does.'

Of course, the tavern erupted into laughter and the red-faced man left in high dudgeon; but I have often reflected since on the status of women and wondered whether we men could be fairer to them. They face the dangers of pregnancy and childbirth, and many succumb. A great many of them live lives of hard work and drudgery; so do their men, it is true, but men have their tavern pleasures and women do not. I am aware that the coffee and tea shops of our cities are filled with women with coins in their purse and time to themselves, but they are not many compared with the mass of their sisters in the alleys and squalid rooms. Most women live their whole lives as property of one man or another, unable or unwilling to complain.

My mind turned to Elisabeth Wolf. Why had she not informed the authorities of her husband's savage treatment of her? Not only had she concealed it, it sounded as if she had actually denied it. Why would a woman do that?

Is it shame? Is it a feeling that if her husband does not love her, she has somehow deserved such shabby treatment? I have heard women say that so long as their husband feeds them, he is entitled to use them as he pleases; but these are somebody's sister, somebody's daughter. So far as I know my father never raised a hand to my mother, but if he had I hope I would have defended her. Wouldn't anyone do the same, if he deserves to be called a man?

I was disturbed in my thoughts by Boudewijn's coughing.

'Are you all right?' I asked.

'I was saying, Master, that the mayor has returned if you wish to speak to him.'

I could hardly avoid it, so I knocked on the door of his chamber and stood respectfully at the threshold.

'Master! How good to see you returned safely to us! How did you fare in Koudekerk?'

'I learned little to the point, but at least I feel comfortable that no member of Elisabeth Wolf's family was responsible for Wolf's death.'

'I can't imagine that there were great lamentations at his passing.'

'Indeed, there were not. Apart from Joost, nobody seems to regret his death very much. Of course, the majority are distressed to think that he was taken before his time, but even the fact of murder does not soften some hearts.'

The mayor rubbed his earlobe in thought. 'We should bury him soon. Even in this cold weather we cannot keep him above ground until the judges come to Leiden.'

'I agree. They could be weeks yet.'

'Oh, not at all, Master! They are coming next Tuesday.'

My heart seemed to simultaneously drop and leap forward in my chest. I had only a few days to prove Jaco's innocence. It was, at least in theory, possible to wait until the day of the trial, but court proceedings at these assizes were very brisk. The judges might dispose of a case in an afternoon, and that left very little room for argumentation. Very few men charged with murder were ever acquitted. My best hope was never to let him come to trial.

'You look pale, Master,' said the mayor. 'Are you still ailing?'

How stupid I had been to waste a whole day going to Koudekerk on a wild goose chase! How wretched to drink too much and lose an entire afternoon as a result! If Jaco Zwart hanged as a result of my indolence, I could never forgive myself. I had been entrusted with his safety and I had failed him. Sara Zwart believed and trusted in me, and I had let her down.

'Some brandy, perhaps?' the mayor suggested.

'No, thank you,' I replied. 'I must forswear strong drink until my work is done.'

The mayor looked extremely concerned. 'Surely you're not going to drink water?' he said.

The water in Oegstgeest was more palatable than that in Leiden, but then the water I had poured into the runnel was purer than Leiden water. The woolworkers wash their fleeces in it and then return it to the water courses, so there is often a layer of wool fat floating on it, and if you have ever smelled a wet sheep you will know what that did for the desirability of the water.

'Forgive me,' I said, 'I should be about my business. I have a man's innocence to prove, and I won't do it sitting here.'

'Perhaps not,' said the mayor, 'but what do you propose to do that is more to the point? Mere activity won't do it. We must make a definite plan.'

The justice of his argument could not be questioned. Clearly just running around for the sake of it would achieve nothing.

'Why not sup with us, have an early night and tackle your quest with renewed vigour in the morning?' he asked.

I could not deny it was tempting, but then so were the offers made by Satan to Our Lord after He had fasted forty days in the wilderness.

'Perhaps Joanna could play for you. Music always soothes away my cares,' the mayor added.

I began to feel even more uncomfortable. If the mayor thought that I was a suitor for his daughter's hand, I must clarify at once that a match was not possible. This was always something of a challenge, because I could not reveal that I was a Catholic priest; I was fairly sure that somewhere in the small print of the law there was something that allowed mayors to burn self-confessed Catholics on the spot if the fancy took them, and the fact that the law was never applied was no comfort, because there is always a first time.

On the other hand, I could not claim that my affections were already engaged because, as my dear grandmother would tell me, my face betrayed me every time I tried to lie.

But perhaps I was worrying unnecessarily. It might be that she was already spoken for. I decided to make gentle and tactful enquiries to set my mind at rest.

'Your daughter plays very well,' I said.

'She does,' beamed her happy father. 'Some lucky fellow will do very well to marry her.'

So much for tact. I could hardly come slowly to the matter now. 'Surely she is too young to commit herself?' I began.

'Hardly,' said the mayor. 'She has seen nearly eighteen years. Plenty of young women are married by her age.'

This was undoubtedly true, especially among the aristocracy and royalty. Only a short while before a girl of nine had been married to a man of forty-three. No doubt she looked older surrounded by her wealth.

'She is a very accomplished and attractive young woman,' I conceded. 'I am sure that there are many seeking her hand. I understand that Oegstgeest has a dearth of young women at present.'

'It does,' the mayor conceded. 'If a village has only half a dozen births a year, and for a few years in succession it has four boys and two girls instead of three of each, the balance is soon upset.'

'Is there no particular boy whom she favours?'

The mayor shook his head vigorously. 'Joanna is not a girl to form opinions of that kind without consulting her parents first. We do not encourage callers, and Joanna rarely goes out.'

'But she is educated, so I had supposed she had gone to school.'

'She did, to the school here in the village, and later the old minister tutored her for a while. She also helped to teach the small children at Sunday School.'

'Is the new minister married?' I asked.

'Ah, I can see where your thoughts lead! No, he is not, but, to be frank, I do not think he will stay with us much longer. The village is too quiet for him.'

It did not seem appropriate to interject that since I was there to investigate a murder, it could hardly be fairly described as "too quiet", so I held my peace.

'I doubt if any woman from these parts would marry a man who saw his future elsewhere, Master; at least, if he were to think of venturing too far afield,' the mayor continued. His eyebrows eloquently conveyed the thought that Leiden would not be too far afield if the right man came along. 'Of course, when he leaves we shall be looking for a young and accomplished man of God to lead our flock here,' the mayor added, adopting a tone of voice that implied that he knew exactly where to seek for one. 'The manse is a very fine house, newly rebuilt not long since, and comfortably furnished.'

If he had suggested an immediate inspection of my new home at this juncture I should not have been surprised. It was time to put a stop to this folly, but I did not want to forfeit his goodwill.

It was at this point that a splendid idea occurred to me. I knew Joanna to be a sensible and intelligent girl. If I could get her on her own I could explain that, while I found her estimable in every way, the age difference of twenty-three years between us, my single-minded devotion to my job, and my inability to keep her on a lecturer's salary (true, but I would say nothing about the savings I had locked in the goldsmith's strongroom) would make her unhappy. She would form this opinion for herself, because it was so obviously correct, and I would regretfully withdraw from the competition for her hand, bloodied but unbowed. If she mentioned any other man, I would praise him enthusiastically and thus escape the snares being laid for me.

Buoyed up by the brilliance of my own stratagem, I resumed my good humour and determined to pass the evening in the guise of a keen but hopelessly inadequate suitor. After all, I told myself, I was not the marrying kind.

As the mayor and I headed towards the door, it opened, and Sara Zwart entered. She dipped in a brief curtsey. 'If I might see Jaco,' she said, 'I have some soup for him.'

Her large eyes looked up at mine. The dark pupils were like bottomless wells into which any man might fall, and the pleading look on her face was so earnest that I felt that I could deny her nothing.

The mayor nodded, and she thanked him and passed by me, offering me the briefest and most tentative of smiles. Unless I came up with an alternative suspect, she would be a widow in just a few days. Who would care for her then?

I have to accept that the alert reader, if I have any, may be confused about my feelings and motives with respect to these women at this point. I was rather conflicted myself. On the one hand, Joanna was apparently available, and an undoubted catch, but I felt compelled to refuse because I was not free to marry. Sara, on the other hand, attracted me greatly, and while inconveniently married at present, by next Tuesday evening she might not be. I could not, however, put out of my mind the moral consideration that if she became free to marry that would be because I had failed to take care of her husband's interests; and I liked Jaco too. All common sense told me that I must put Sara out of my mind and stop fantasising; but what has common sense to do with the heart?

I would have expected the Gerrits family to be weary of my repeated appearances, but I was again received with every courtesy. Mevrouw Gerrits went at once to the kitchen to make the necessary arrangements with the cook, and then returned to dress the dining table; meanwhile, the mayor summoned his daughter to keep me company by the fireplace before suddenly "remembering" some urgent business that would keep both himself and his wife occupied for at least ten minutes and leaving the room with a smug smile.

Whatever had been whispered between them in the few moments' speech that they had shared as Joanna was brought downstairs, it was clear that it had unnerved Joanna somewhat, and her convulsive squeezing of her handkerchief gave me some idea what that might have been. She looked as if her smile was extremely forced.

My late father used to say that tact was the brother of lying, by which I assume that he meant that it may slip easily into dissimulation. This may explain why I am no good at it. I have no skill at all in diplomatic language, and despite my best efforts to ease gently into my subject and have myself ruled out as a potential suitor, I contrived to set off on precisely the wrong foot.

'Your father tells me that none of the local young men have paid court to you,' I said.

Joanna was too moved to speak, and just shook her head.

'I find that hard to understand, given your obvious accomplishments, juffrouw.'

At this point I thought I heard a little sob, but she may just have been clearing her throat.

This one-sided conversation was very taxing. I find it difficult to speak about myself, but I had run out of things to say. Thinking to ease the tension a little, I tried a self-deprecating remark. 'I am unattached myself. I'm afraid young ladies have found me rather uninteresting.'

I could have sworn that she made to run out of the room, but then remembered that her father had instructed her to keep me company.

'This is awkward,' I admitted, and then realised that I had said my thought out loud. This is a bad habit that I have, often evident at times of mental stress.

'Master,' said Joanna, trying very hard not to make eye contact yet speaking very earnestly, 'I hope you will not think ill of me if I say that marriage is far from my mind and that I think myself too young to have the responsibility of a household. I do not think that I am fitted to care for a husband as a good man would deserve.'

Thank goodness for that, I thought, and tried hard to look disappointed, but then I realised that this merely made Joanna even more uncomfortable than she already was.

'Juffrouw,' I said in a low voice, 'I think we are of one mind in this, but I should be loath to disappoint your parents who have been so kind to me. What are we going to say?'

'If my father supports your suit, I am bound as a dutiful daughter to accept it,' she wailed. 'You must persuade him that you find me unattractive.'

'I cannot,' I protested. 'First, because he would be offended and second, because it's not true.'

Joanna looked up at me, wild-eyed at the horror of my honesty.

'I mean,' I stuttered, 'that I have no skill in counterfeiting these things.'

By this stage, the poor young woman looked utterly confused.

'What I'm trying to say is, I think, that if I were the marrying kind, which I am, except that circumstances … well, never mind that … you are exactly the sort of young woman for whom I would press my suit, and my failure to do so is not the result of not wanting … it's not that you're at all unattractive.' I gulped. This was not going well. 'I had hoped that you would tell me that there was someone else and that my courting was futile,' I admitted.

'I can't just invent a suitor to ease your conscience, Master,' she protested.

'No, no, I suppose not. I suppose I must be the one to do so,' I murmured, then remembered an impediment to such a ruse, 'except that I have already told your father there isn't anyone.'

I found my mind conjuring up a scene in which I knelt before my Bishop and tried to explain why I, a priest of the Holy Catholic Church, had found it necessary to marry. Every possible justification my fevered brain could think of sounded remarkably unconvincing even to me, so goodness knows what the Bishop would think. I wasn't even able to explain to myself how I had stumbled into this mess in the first place. Maybe the best answer was to castrate myself without further ado.

Castration! Abelard! The links fired across my mind like arrows speeding to their target. Abelard was castrated by Héloïse's uncle so that he could not marry her. I wouldn't actually have to castrate myself, just tell the mayor that it had been done! He might reasonably ask why I had only just thought to mention it, but as a bar to marriage it was pretty final, I thought; and I could say that I had not volunteered it out of shame.

Joanna was staring fixedly at my face as if trying to read my thoughts, though I am sure that even in the midst of fever she would never have come up with the right answer. But this explanation needed to be fleshed out, for which time was necessary.

'Juffrouw,' I said, 'I may have the answer, but we need to delay matters. Shall we say that I have invited you and your mother to visit me in Leiden when all this terrible matter is behind us, because we agree that this is not the time to speak of such things while a man's life hangs in the balance?'

She nodded uncertainly. This might be a delaying tactic, but I could see that to her it still seemed like a step along a path that she did not wish to tread. Moreover, I do not think that I had convinced her that I was just as keen to avoid marriage.

Her parents had still not returned to the room, and I decided to change the subject to give us both a chance to recover our equilibrium.

'How well do you know Joost Wolf?' I asked.

Joanna reddened. 'We went to school together,' she said. 'We are of an age, you see.'

'And then, I understand, you were tutored at home when school finished for you both.'

'That is so, Master. Joost went to work for his father.'

'I understand that he is fond of alehouse company,' I said.

'No, Master!' Joanna protested vehemently.

Now, I am the first to grant that I do not have great skill in the arts of conversation, and that the subtle insinuations of polite company often pass me by, but the strength of her objection to my suggestion conveyed to me the idea that I had missed something.

'No?'

'No! Joost is not a drinker,' she asserted before collecting herself and adding, 'to the best of my knowledge, anyway.'

'But you don't go to the inn, so how could you know?' I said. 'I'm sorry, it was an unfair comment to make. No doubt you were defending him from a proper sense that I should not make such assertions to one who could not judge the truth of them.'

She appeared mollified. 'And I am sorry too,' she said. 'As you rightly say, I cannot know the truth of it, so I should not have voiced my silly opinion on something beyond my knowledge.'

Her mother then pushed the door open very slowly, as if giving us the chance to disentangle ourselves from an embrace, and seemed rather disappointed that neither of us looked flustered as she entered. 'I'm so sorry to have left you for so long,' she said. 'I hope you found something to speak about?'

'Yes,' said Joanna at once, which would have been fine if I had not said 'No' simultaneously. No wonder mevrouw Gerrits looked confused.

'I mean that your daughter has been enchanting, but I'm afraid this terrible affair has left me rather distracted and I have not been good company for her,' I declared.

'Well, never mind,' said mevrouw Gerrits, slowly smoothing out the folds of her gown as she sat. 'No doubt you will soon resolve that matter and life in Oegstgeest will return to normality.'

Her faith in me was clear, and I was in little doubt what "normality" would encompass.

I gulped again.

CHAPTER EIGHTEEN

It is some time since I read the *Divine Comedy* of Dante Alighieri, but I am fairly sure that somewhere in there he will have described an evening of hell such as I experienced that night.

There was nothing wrong with the food or the company, though Joanna seemed in low spirits, which her father seemed inclined to ascribe to her reluctant acquiescence in his wedding plans. Invited to play the flute after dinner, she played a couple of pieces but without any passion or, indeed, overmuch fidelity to the melody, and then asked leave to go to her chamber because she was tired.

'Of course,' said her father. 'I know that Master Mercurius wishes to be up betimes in the morning too, so perhaps we should all retire.'

I gladly assented, and a few minutes later was lying on my bed, still fully dressed, thinking what a complete fool I was. Not only had I ensnared myself in a potential marriage that I could not go through with, but the pretext I had found to escape from it, which had seemed so perfect and conclusive a couple of hours before, now appeared to me like the desperate ravings of a lunatic. If I could not lie about having a previous girlfriend, what on earth possessed me to think that I could successfully concoct a story about having been unmanned somehow? It was unlikely that Gerrits would insist upon an examination by a surgeon, but if he did my deception would be laid bare, so the tale I was composing mentally subtly changed from one of castration to one involving an unspecified accident which had left me unable to consummate the marriage. I had heard of such things, often involving a kick from a horse. Since my grandfather had been a blacksmith it was not altogether improbable, though the fact that I had presumably gone nearly thirty years without mentioning it to anyone might tell against me. And I was not exactly clear what the horse had to do to make the story credible; but then the horse was not going to be called as a witness.

I climbed wearily to my feet and walked over to the window. Snow was still falling in slow, large flakes, yet against the wall of the house opposite I could see a figure wrapped in a large cloak huddled up for warmth. How sad it was that there were men and women compelled to walk abroad in such weather for lack of a place of their own to call home!

I turned back towards my bed, intending to add him or her to my prayers, when something caused me to look again. I could not see the face because the figure — a man, surely — wore a hat with a broad brim, but I was sure that he was looking up at me, and during a fleeting moment when the clouds parted and the moon shone brighter, I had the distinct impression that I was once more looking at the face of Joost Wolf.

I pulled back to the side of the window, hoping to observe without being observed, and it was then I realised that the added light was not from the moon, but from a candle or lantern which was in the room next door.

And suddenly my eyes were opened.

I did not sleep much that night. My brain was far too active, as it needed to be because it was trying to make links where I had neglected to look for facts. Trying to solve the murder at this point was like attempting to make bricks without straw; or, indeed, clay.

However, I now had a line of attack in front of me. I had no idea where it led, or what it meant, but I could see that it must be important somehow.

In the morning I dressed very early and waited in my room for sounds of movement. The various doors opened and closed, and after a while I heard feminine steps on the stairs. About ten minutes later, the same steps ascended again and approached my door. At the first tap on the wood, I pulled the door open.

'Step inside a minute, please,' I whispered.

'Master! It would not be proper!' Joanna protested.

'You don't want me to ask you what I must ask in front of others,' I said urgently, gently taking her by the arm and drawing her within.

She stepped inside and pushed the door almost shut while still allowing herself a speedy escape.

'Why didn't you tell me Joost Wolf was in love with you?' I asked.

'I don't know that he is,' she claimed.

'Come, Joanna, I have seen him in the street under these windows more than once. I thought he was lying in wait for me, but now I realise he stands there and looks up at your window. He comes to the inn but then he soon leaves and comes here, doesn't he? And most nights when I'm not here, he is able to exchange a few words because you open your window to him. That is why he looked with such an evil eye upon me; not, as I thought, because I was making no progress in finding the killer of his father, but because my presence in this chamber thwarted him of his nightly conversation with you.'

'No, it's not like that!' she hissed.

'I saw the light in your window last night. No doubt you were signalling to him, though you had to remain silent. Did you blow him sweet kisses?'

Joanna quickly put down the jug of hot water and ran from the room. I heard her door shut, followed by the sound of muffled sobbing as she cried into her pillow.

By the time I descended to breakfast, the atmosphere had changed somewhat. I had the strong feeling that the family would be happier if I were not there. Either Joanna had said something, or they had detected that something had transpired to make her unhappy. As I left, I therefore made a point of thanking them profusely for their hospitality and assuring them that I did not expect to burden them again.

'Does that mean, Master, that you are close to resolving this affair?' the mayor asked.

'I can say only that I have made a significant advance in my understanding,' I replied, 'but it remains to be seen whether it leads directly to a conclusion.'

I hoped that he would not ask me what I meant by that, because I was unsure myself, but I had a strong sentiment that there was something about my discovery that was important. On the other hand, since it seemed to have no bearing at all on the events of the afternoon when Wolf died, perhaps I was deluding myself. It would not be the first time.

We are all tempted to construe facts to fit our hopes and desires. I had sometimes observed at the University that when the Rector was asked a question, he was adept at making a non-committal remark which satisfied both sides of the argument yet which, when subjected to deeper analysis, actually said nothing at all. Asked, for example, whether a faculty would be permitted to accept more students in the following year, he would say that he was giving very active consideration to the suggestion, which the questioner would take to mean an affirmative answer, but in fact he had said no such thing. Maybe I was doing the same in the matter of Joost's pursuit of Joanna Gerrits, who, I could now see clearly, was far too young for me. If I were to pay court to a lady, it would have to be a woman more nearly approaching my own age. Someone around the age of Sara Zwart, to take an example that just happened to occur to me.

I had abandoned any intention to fabulate an account of whatever incredible accident might have left me unable to procreate. Avoiding offence was no longer possible, given that the offence had already been taken. The best way to rehabilitate myself in the mayor's eyes was to solve this crime speedily and efficiently, so that is the goal that I pursued with renewed energy.

It dawned on me that one person to whom I should undoubtedly already have spoken was the minister of Oegstgeest, this young fellow who was apparently on the verge of leaving. I walked over to the manse to present my compliments, not with any expectation of advancing my enquiry but out of a sense of brotherly duty.

To my surprise, I already knew him. Bartholomeus de Jong had been a student of mine about ten years earlier at the University, where he stood out from his undergraduate colleagues by relentlessly staying awake during my lectures, handing in his assignments on time and occasionally adopting one of the lines of argument I suggested. After completion of the *Artes*, he had enrolled for a theology degree and done very well, considering that he did not come from a family of the cloth. The top marks most years were won by men who were themselves the sons and grandsons of ministers and who had therefore had some instruction at home before arriving at Leiden. This is not to say that our tuition was worthless, but they were better able to use it to the full. De Jong had lacked this advantage, but had demonstrated a keen intelligence, a certain degree of humility which, believe me, is not often seen in our younger students, and a remarkable facility with the biblical languages.

He greeted me warmly and invited me into his study. Although it was early in the day, I accepted a glass of wine, vowing to myself that I would not allow it to be refilled.

'I am delighted to see you, Master,' De Jong announced. 'It has been a long time.'

'I had no idea you were so close at hand,' I replied. 'I wonder that we have not seen you about the University.'

'I visit the library occasionally,' De Jong replied, 'and I attend some of the public lectures when my duties here permit which, sadly, is not as often as I would like.'

'Gossip has it that you do not expect to be here much longer,' I suggested.

De Jong laughed gently. 'For once, gossip has the right of it,' he said. 'But I should not like it to be thought that there is any dissatisfaction on my part with this village. Rather, it is because I have lately become convinced that my talents, such as they are, should be directed towards another object. God has given me a certain ability with languages, and I have been invited to take up a post as a missionary minister in the East Indies. It is not congenial work to many of our countrymen, Master, but I am convinced that to convert the savages we must preach to them directly in their own language, and I expect to do that. I have been learning Javanese in my free time to equip myself for the task. And, of course, I have no family ties here, being unmarried.'

'I wish you well in your endeavours,' I replied. At least this fellow proposed to convert by persuasion rather than by bribes or threats. 'It is remiss of me not to have called upon you earlier. You may know that I am here to assist the mayor in investigating the death of one Franciscus Wolf.'

De Jong inclined his head. 'So I understand. It is a horrible business.'

'Indeed it is. Did you know the Wolf family?'

De Jong swirled his wine in his glass as if this action might assist his cogitation. 'Say, rather, that I knew of them, rather than knew them. The wife, of course, had expired during my predecessor's time, though he told me something of the history and his suspicions in that regard. In my time Franciscus Wolf has given the church a wide berth. The son, however, was an occasional attender.'

'Joost came to church?' I regretted my tone as soon as I uttered the sentence, because it sounded as if I had written Joost off as a pagan unbeliever.

'He did. He would slip in at the back and leave promptly at the conclusion, though occasionally as I said farewell to people at the door I would see him loitering along the street. I may be wrong, but I think he may have had tender feelings for a young lady.'

'Joanna Gerrits?'

De Jong smiled. 'My, but you have informed yourself well in such a short time!'

This puzzled me. If I had seen this, albeit belatedly, and the minister, a man of discretion, had observed it, why hadn't anyone else? There was only one way to find out. 'If you could see that,' I said, 'why hasn't anyone else said it to me?'

'I don't know,' De Jong shrugged. 'Maybe they thought the notion of such a union fantastical and therefore dismissed it from their heads as even a remote possibility. Do you recall the year the circus came to Leiden?'

I did. Circuses are infrequent visitors to my home town, but the circus of which De Jong spoke was unusual in having a menagerie. 'You refer to the escapee?'

'Yes,' chuckled De Jong. 'Many people must have seen that monkey but because they did not know that one was in Leiden, let alone that it had escaped, they ascribed its depredations to small children. Perhaps the same sense overpowered people here about Joost's feelings for juffrouw Gerrits; and, of course, he did nothing to forward them.'

You might ask why I did not correct him on this point, but it is in the nature of ministers of religion to disclose only what must be shared. Confidentiality is a matter of habit with us.

'Did you have any sense that his feelings were reciprocated?' I enquired.

'No, I saw no sign of that. The Gerrits family are keen to be thought above the common people. They stand firmly on their dignity; and, to be fair, they are assiduous in public service and charity, and prudent in their business dealings. No taint of scandal or ill-living attaches to them.'

'They have been very kind to me,' I agreed. 'I have been accommodated, in fact, spoiled, on several occasions. I fear I may have caused them some displeasure this morning.'

De Jong did not ask. If I wanted to tell him, I would tell; if not, I would not.

'I am afraid that they may have formed the notion that I would pay suit to their daughter,' I explained.

'I guessed as much. They broached the subject with me too, not in any openly ambitious way, but I noted the hints that ministers here are usually married and that the salary that the church was paying me would amply support a larger household.'

I was, I admit, a little put out by this. It is one thing to chase after a minister, but to discover that Joanna's parents have been indiscriminately trying to marry their daughter into the church, and that there was nothing special about me, was wounding to some degree.

'I confess that I was uncomfortable with it,' I admitted, while saying nothing about the conversation I had shared with Joanna earlier that morning.

'Think nothing of it. As soon as I am replaced, they'll be circling around the new man. You see, a family here cannot rise further than the Gerrits. They are pre-eminent in trade, but reluctant to move to an enlarged sphere for fear of a backward step. Oh, Gerrits has made a few deals in Leiden, I have no doubt, but here he is the champion cock. Elsewhere, he would be just one of the roost. If, however, he could marry his daughter to a professional man, his standing would be elevated. I assure you that any of the lecturers at Leiden would serve his purpose just as well. He will already be telling himself that you were not as high as he might have aimed. I mean no offence; he would think it whether it were true or not. It would be balm to his wound.'

'Did you speak to Joost?'

'Once or twice, in a very general way. I expressed surprise that he should attend a church despite his father's well-known views on us. It showed, I thought, that the young man had sound principles. The bible instructs us to honour our father and our mother, Master, and not to oppose them, yet I think Joost Wolf did well when he disregarded his father's opinion to join in our fellowship. Am I to say that he sinned by doing so?'

'He seems to have honoured his mother,' I replied.

'Such a sad story,' De Jong answered. 'I cannot say I know the truth of it, for all those who speak about it have already formed their prejudices. There were allegations, which my predecessor shared, that Wolf in some way contributed to or caused his wife's passing. Whether his strident opposition to the church stemmed from his feelings of guilt, or from a sense that he had been unfairly judged, God only knows.'

'As He knows all things,' I replied, thinking, not for the first time, that if He cared to share some of that knowledge He would make my job a lot easier.

'So He does. Joost said that he was very aware that his home was the last house in the village and therefore the furthest from the centre. He felt very cut off, and there were no people of his own age nearby.'

'Mevrouw De Boer employs two young men.'

'Yes, but they don't live there and, although they have changed over the years, they have always kept company with each other rather than with Joost. Of course, the current pair are the first who have been of an age with him, the previous ones being rather older than him.'

'What do you make of them?' I asked.

'Gillis is a conscientious young man, probably the more intelligent of the pair. Gerrit is a rough diamond, but with a good heart. I would vouch for both of them as honest youths. Gerrit is sometimes very literal.'

'I'm sorry, I don't follow.'

'He doesn't seem to grasp parables very well. I remember preaching on the parable of the lilies of the field, and he asked me afterwards why they would put clothes on flowers. I had to explain that when the Bible says that "even Solomon in all his splendour was not arrayed as one of these" it doesn't mean that the lilies wore clothes. I'm not sure he grasped it fully even after my explanation. But that kind of innocence is quite touching. I would not rob him of it.'

I rubbed my cheek in thought. Something was niggling at my brain, the sense that there was an obvious question that I ought to be asking if only I could think what it might be. 'What of Jaco Zwart? Do you believe that he could kill a man?'

'Oh, yes,' answered De Jong, to my surprise. 'Not in cold blood, perhaps, but in a passion, certainly. Do you not think that most men can, Master? How many of those are convicted of such a thing though their neighbours declare that they had no idea that they were capable of it? It is a melancholy truth that most of us can kill if we have a knife in our hand and the Devil in our blood.'

'Are we to ascribe evil to the Devil, then?' I asked, only half-seriously. I knew what the answer would be.

'The Devil may be very real, Master, but we have our free will. We can, and should, resist his promptings. For, if we do not, the world swiftly descends into chaos.'

I decided not to answer him for, if I spoke my true thoughts, I would swiftly reveal my Catholicism or, at least, my dissatisfaction with Reformed teaching. I grew up believing that God knew even before He created mankind which of us would be saved and which would descend to Hell. What about free will, I hear my students cry, if I give them long enough and one or two hints? If our actions are foreordained, we can do nothing different, so why should we be criticised for them? Whoever murdered Wolf, God ordained that he would be a murderer, and therefore that he should hang for it, and there was nothing at all that the poor fellow could do about it.

The standard answer that Reformed theologians give is that just because God knew what we would choose doesn't mean we didn't have a choice. None of us know what God has decided for us, therefore we strive as if the decision had not been made; and while a minister might think that nothing he does is going to change things, he must make the effort to exhort people to holy living because God has ordained that it will be successful — or not.

I need not say that this struck me as a doctrine that was short on hope; so much so that it became a barrier for me. Simple compassion led me to prefer the Catholic teaching that did not set a limit on the capacity of Heaven, and in time that is why I was moved to convert. I admit, however, that I had no thoughts of becoming a priest until the bishop offered to ordain me.

I am not sure that I have ever met an evil person, you see. I have met people who have done evil things, but there but for the Grace of God go I. Adherence to the law may not be a good yardstick, for if a man steals a loaf of bread to feed his children, is that evil? God said thou shalt not steal, and that is good enough reason to punish, I suppose, but would he condemn a man who stood before him and said "I sacrificed myself for the sake of others"?

It was a sombre thought, and I think I must have conveyed my gloom to De Jong, who sat patiently as this passed through my mind, and said nothing.

'I must leave you in peace,' I said. 'You have given me something to think about.'

'I wish you well in finding the killer of Franciscus Wolf,' De Jong replied. 'He was not a likeable man, I'm afraid, though that isn't a reason to kill him.'

'Whoever did it obviously thought it was,' I replied.

Or did they?

CHAPTER NINETEEN

Sometimes I think it would do me some good if a friend were to take me aside and give me a good scourging to cure my arrogance and knock some sense into me. I had been flailing around for days when the answer was staring me in the face.

Let us return to the murderer's trinity — means, motive and opportunity. Maybe anyone could have had the means, because they may well have used one of Wolf's own knives. It was hard to imagine anyone walking around the streets with a weapon of the sort that had been used, not knowing whom they might meet on the way. I had been thinking that the motive was hatred of Wolf, but maybe the killing was simply instrumental — he was killed because he was in the way, or in the wrong place at the wrong time. The soldier who storms a castle does not hate the sentries at the gates; he kills them because it is necessary to do so to achieve his goal. My conversation with De Jong at least suggested that I should examine this aspect.

Then there was opportunity. The one person whom we knew had the opportunity was Jaco Zwart. The difficulty was that he was not a man to lose his temper, and he had shrugged off many past events, so why should he react violently to this one? Clearly I needed to do some deep and uninterrupted thinking. The obvious place to do so was the church, but I preferred the inn.

With a tankard in front of me and a clean — well, relatively clean — table on which to spread out my papers, I began re-reading the notes I had made on each discussion in turn. I must have missed something, unless Jaco really was guilty, which I doubted.

When I found it, I could not believe that I had overlooked it. I must have looked a fool, particularly because my tankard was halfway to my mouth and I let the contents slop over the side.

I turned back to the previous page and began reading the passage again. If I had correctly noted Gerrit Hoet's testimony, the answer had been before me all along. First, however, I had to check exactly what he had said.

I swallowed the remaining ale and paid for my drink before plucking up my gown and breaking into a run. It must have looked rather unseemly, but I did not want doubts to overtake me again. Arriving at the home of mevrouw De Boer, I briefly asked her leave to speak to the young men once more, which she gladly gave.

They were undoubtedly surprised to see me there, and doubly so because I was probably quite red from the unaccustomed effort, but they greeted me respectfully.

'Gillis, Gerrit,' I said, 'I want you to indulge me for a moment. I want to re-enact the events of that afternoon when Wolf was killed. Could you show me where you were standing when you first became aware of the commotion?'

The two youths thought for a moment before striding across the ground to take up their positions. Gillis was slightly nearer the house, Gerrit more towards the end of the garden, the two of them about twenty paces apart.

'Now, what caused you to look up?'

Gerrit leaned on his hoe and frowned. 'I don't think anything caused it, Master. You just stand up from time to time and you see things.'

'So what did you see? Who was where?'

Gerrit pointed down the slight slope. 'Joost was under the roof overhang filling the buckets with feed. The pig was hoping there would be some titbits for him.'

'Then you heard the argument?'

'Yes. We could only hear that there was an argument, not much of what was said. But then mijnheer Wolf's voice became louder, and we could hear his side of the argument more clearly.'

'When we spoke the other day, you said that mevrouw De Boer came out to you, and it was then that Joost ran round the house.'

'That's right.'

'And shortly afterwards Joost called for help because his father had been stabbed.'

'Yes.'

I was trying to picture the scene in my head, but I was missing one key element. 'Where was the pig?'

Gillis and Gerrit looked at each other, then at me.

'The pig, Master?' said Gillis.

'Yes. Where was the pig? You said he was waiting expectantly beside Joost when he was preparing some food, so he must have been at the back of the house. So when did he go to the front?'

The two youths were at a loss.

'I don't know, Master. I can't say I was looking at the pig,' Gillis answered.

I walked down the hill to the Wolfs' house. Joost was hammering a fence post into the ground at the back when I found him.

'It's a shame that wasn't fixed a few weeks ago,' I said. 'It would have prevented a lot of trouble if the fence had been sound.'

'The pig's alright if you know how to handle him,' Joost said sullenly.

I nodded to show I understood. 'Can we have a few words?' I said.

I had no idea what words exactly would be suitable to the occasion, but I wanted to be absolutely sure of my ground before speaking to the mayor.

'I suppose so,' said Joost. 'Have you found out what happened yet?'

'I think so,' I said. 'It took me a while, but in the end it has become clearer. It wasn't so much the sequence of events as the reason why, but now I think I know that too. It's a really sad story. Why not sit down while I tell you what I know, and you can help me fill in the gaps?'

Joost found a stool and sat on it. I preferred to stand.

'It's a strange thing,' I said, 'but the human mind likes tidiness. So much so that when a bit of the story sticks out, it prefers to hammer it back into place and convince itself that there really isn't an awkward point rather than consider too carefully why something sticks out. And that's what I did wrong. We had abundant witnesses all telling the same story, so I accepted the story as true and consistent, and from that it was clear that Jaco Zwart must have killed your father. Nobody else could have done it.'

'I'm glad you can see that,' Joost replied.

'But there were two things that should have made me question that account. The first was that mevrouw Hoeks was adamant that the pig was not in front of the house. Well, then, to stab it, Jaco would either have had to do so before he returned it, but nobody suggested that he had done that, or he must have come round the back of the house, but nobody saw him there. Gerrit and Gillis were clear that before the argument started, the pig was at the back of the house, apparently quite comfortable.

'The second was the timing. Gerrit was sure that it was while mevrouw De Boer was speaking to him that he saw you run to the front of the house. Now, that cannot have been immediately after the women saw your father and Jaco arguing in the lane, because mevrouw De Boer had time to walk up the lane to her house, put her bag down, take off her coat and bonnet, don her apron, and walk out to the back field where the boys were. So whatever caused you to run round to the front, it can't have been the argument between Jaco and your father, because Jaco had marched off while the women could still see him. Gerrit thought that you then found the body of your father and ran up the road shouting for help. But mevrouw De Boer had been with them giving them instructions and checking on their work, and she had walked back to the house and was in her kitchen when she heard you shouting, so Gerrit must be wrong. The timing won't allow him to be right, do you see?'

'No, Master, I don't see anything,' Joost grumbled.

'Joost, I saw you outside the mayor's house on two separate occasions. I know that you went there to speak to Joanna Gerrits. She is a very attractive young lady, isn't she?'

'You don't need a university education to see that.'

'No, you don't. In fact, you were in love with her, weren't you?'

Joost did not reply.

'You'd known her a long time. She was friendly to you. And it was time for you to start looking for a wife. But her father would never permit it, even if you persuaded her.'

'He treats us like we were something he stepped in, but he's no better than us. It's not that long ago that mijnheer Gerrits was trading second-hand lengths of rope, but he puts on his airs and graces and talks down to the likes of me.'

'And when you spoke about it to your father, what did he say?'

Joost suddenly seemed very interested in his hands, to which he devoted his entire attention.

'What did he say, Joost?' I pressed him.

'He said I should forget about Joanna Gerrits, because women like her weren't going to lower themselves to marry scum like us.'

'But she was friendly, wasn't she?'

'She never said she wouldn't marry me. We just didn't get round to it.'

It was as I had suspected. What Joost thought was the conversation of lovers was, in Joanna's eyes, just a chat between friends. She was too young to understand the way his mind was tending, and he was too inexperienced in the world to realise that he had misinterpreted those brief colloquies at the window.

'So the idea came to you that if you had some money, if you were somebody in the world, nobody could deny your right to court Joanna Gerrits. But there was only one way you could get wealth. You didn't stab your father because you hated him; you did it because he was in the way.'

'He held me back! If he'd run this farm properly, we'd have had a nice income. But he couldn't afford to pay anyone else to work for him, not even someone like Gerrit or Gillis. I'd still be working for him when he was an old man, and we'd be scratching a living. No woman would ever marry me, given she'd be near starving most of the time. There was barely food for two, let alone three. And I wouldn't bring a decent woman into this house, not after what he did to Mother.'

Joost's shoulders shook as he broke into sobs and wiped his nose on his sleeve. 'She was a good woman, a saintly woman, but he used her so badly!' he cried. 'And the way he spoke about women and what they were good for, if I'd brought a woman into this house I couldn't trust him not to manhandle her. I said I loved Joanna Gerrits and he said I'd never get her legs apart, she was so tight-arsed. He didn't know her, but he was vile about her.'

'Then when the women came into view, you saw your chance. You cut the pig and told your father that Jaco Zwart must have done it. You knew your father would start an argument with Jaco, so you kept out of the way, then, as soon as your father returned you were lying in wait. You stabbed him, waited just long enough to be sure that he was beyond recovery, then ran around shouting for help. When people came to you, you didn't give a clear story, so by the time they realised what was wrong and made their way down the lane, your father had breathed his last. And very cleverly you didn't point the finger at Jaco for a while, so he wouldn't be sure where he was when it happened and he would have had time to dispose of the knife he'd used. Where is it, by the way?'

'Never you mind.'

'I'm sorry, Joost, but I have to denounce you to the mayor in order to save Jaco. I can't do anything else.'

Joost stood up. 'You've got it all figured out, haven't you, Master? Well, you're a clever man. But you're not clever enough to come here in company. What you know may never get said to the mayor.'

So saying, he rushed towards me with the mallet he had been using to hammer in the fence post. I had anticipated that he might not come quietly, but I had hoped that by remaining standing and being a few paces away at all times, I would be able to run to the safety of someone's house. I had forgotten two things; first, the nearest houses belonged to a woman whose man was currently in jail, and a widow, and second, that running in a clerical gown is not easy on a good road, and almost impossible in the slimy confines of a farmyard. As I tried to run away, I slipped and fell headlong in something filthy.

Needless to say, I had no intention of lying there bemoaning my dirty state while Joost rearranged my skull with his hammer, but getting up was quite tricky. I ducked my head down and took a fearsome blow to the shoulder and another to the middle of my back before I managed to roll under the roof overhang and seize a plank which I held in front of me to ward off the blows.

Joost's hammer splintered the top of the plank, and the next blow would have broken my fingers had I not had the presence of mind to remove my hand, but that caused the plank to drop to the ground. I put my arms over my head to try to protect myself, so I cannot give an eye-witness account of what happened next, but there was a loud thud very close to me followed by a groan, and I instinctively turned my back against the final blow that I knew was about to come.

Instead, hands lifted me up and I heard concerned voices.

'Are you all right, Master?' asked Gillis.

I peeped through my fingers and saw Gerrit Hoet kneeling on Joost's back. Joost was dazed. I learned later that Gerrit and Gillis had seen me talking to Joost and realised quicker than I did that Joost was reaching for the mallet. Gerrit had hurdled fences and hedges and at the crucial moment had slammed Joost face first into the wall of the house. Gillis, meanwhile, had tried to pull me away from danger. I was deeply indebted to them both.

Gerrit and Gillis bound Joost securely and led him to the town hall. The look on Boudewijn's face as we entered was quite indescribable. Whether the cause of his astonishment was the sight of Joost in bonds or the state of my clothing, I cannot say, but he took one look and ran off down the street, returning shortly followed by a very flustered and ruddy mayor.

'What is the meaning of this?' the mayor gasped.

'Perhaps we can secure Joost Wolf somewhere and I will explain.'

The mayor gave Boudewijn the order to bring Jaco downstairs and replace him with Joost.

'Master, you are hurt!' he said.

I attempted to make light of it, but false bravery is not my strong point and I think the mayor concluded that I must have received a blow to the head that had separated me temporarily from reality.

Boudewijn brought water so that I could at least wash my face, and my gown was hung up to dry so that Boudewijn could brush it later. The mayor poured wine for me and himself, but the others preferred beer, which Boudewijn dispensed, having first rummaged around for four beakers.

We sat in a semi-circle, though Jaco preferred to stand after a few days of being chained, which was understandable. The mayor was behind his desk, Boudewijn at his smaller desk as usual, Gerrit and Gillis either side of me.

'If you feel up to it, Master, perhaps you can explain what has happened,' said the mayor, 'for I confess myself utterly bemused.'

'That is not surprising,' I answered, 'for until a few hours ago, I was bewildered myself. And I am not sure that I can give a unified, coherent explanation, but I will try.

'It all begins with the recognition that all the evidence we had appeared to condemn Jaco. He was there, he had a public disagreement with Franciscus Wolf, and there were witnesses to that whose testimony was unimpeachable. To counter that, we had only the belief expressed by many that Jaco would not do such a thing, but we all know that any man may act rashly at times.

'I had some dead ends. We never found the knife, and the trip to Koudekerk achieved less than I had hoped. At most, it showed that news of Wolf's death had not reached there, so it was unlikely that Elisabeth's family had taken their revenge for her death. The witnesses offered the same story, which seemed to lead to one inescapable conclusion. I confess that I thought I had run out of ideas and, therefore, of any hope to save Jaco from the gallows.

'Then I began thinking about apophatic theology. That's not important now,' I said, to the visible relief of those present. 'But in the process of thinking about how we think, I realised that my methodology was suspect. You see, when we hear stories that are nearly identical, our nature is to try to harmonise them. We concentrate on what unites them, and therefore we construct one narrative that leads to one conclusion. That is what we had done with the many witnesses in this case. I had tried to envision mentally how they could fit together, and because that was my intention I was able to do it. But what if I concentrated on the parts of the story that were not common to them all? What if I looked at the parts that stuck out?

'Re-reading the testimonies of all the witnesses one after the other, I noticed an incongruity. Once he returned the pig to Wolf, Jaco was never seen in the same place as the pig again. He cannot, therefore, have cut the pig. Unless Franciscus Wolf did it himself, the only plausible perpetrator was Joost. This is where I regret I may cause you some personal pain and anxiety, mijnheer mayor.'

I paused to take a drink and allow the mayor to prepare himself for bad news.

'Twice while I was sheltering under your roof, I happened to glance out of the bedroom window and saw Joost Wolf outside. I thought he was annoyed with me for questioning the guilt of Jaco, but then it became clear that he was in the habit of speaking to your daughter through her bedroom window. I hasten to add that there was no impropriety. Indeed, I believe your daughter was only being friendly to a boy she had known a long time; but Joost did not take it that way. He thought it was evidence that she may agree to a deeper relationship.'

It seemed appropriate not to delve too deeply into the exact nature of that relationship, but it was clear from the faces of Gillis and Gerrit that they, at least, knew what I meant.

'I confess that my next step was largely based on supposition. If Joost thought that your daughter Joanna could be won, what would he need to do to entice her? The obvious question was how they would live; and knowing the poor state of the farm, that could never happen while Franciscus was running it. Of course, Joost could leave him, but he would go without a guilder to his name. But what if the farm were in Joost's hands? With energy it might be built up again, especially if neighbours offered help and charity. It could, in time, provide Joost and Joanna with as good a living as, say, Jaco and Sara Zwart enjoy. But there was only one way that Joost could lay his hands on it.

'I verified the point about the pig with Gillis and Gerrit here, and then marched down the lane to confront Joost. It is just as well I did, because if these two young men had not been to hand I doubt I would be telling this tale now.'

I described what had transpired at the Wolfs' house, with some added detail from Gerrit. At the end, the mayor sat as if stupefied. Silence filled the air for some time.

'I think,' said the mayor at last, 'that I must have some words with my daughter.'

CHAPTER TWENTY

Jaco was released from his chains, and, after my gown had been well brushed, I walked with him to his home, where Sara was overjoyed to see him. It dawned on me as I watched their reunion that no woman would ever look at me the way Sara looked at Jaco, nor kiss me the way she kissed her husband. They went well together. It was better this way, I told myself.

The mayor had offered me a payment to acknowledge my help, but I declined. I did not need the money, and in any event it had been Sara Zwart who had asked me to become involved. I must also confess that I did not feel that I had really earned any reward, so I thanked him for the offer and for his generous hospitality and took my leave.

Since Joost's attack on me was regarded as a confession of guilt, his appearance in court on the following Tuesday was only for sentencing. Strictly speaking, the mayor and his council could have pronounced sentence themselves, but they chose to present the case to the assize judge. That is not unusual; mayors may have to live with the relatives of the condemned. The conclusion was inevitable, and although I tried to argue that he was too young to know what he was doing or that the cruelty of his father had impaired his sense of right and wrong, I failed to prevent Joost being sentenced to death. As the murderer of his father, he was also sentenced to have the offending hand cut off, but as a concession to his youth the judge allowed that to be done after he was hanged rather than before.

Joost was returned to his confinement to await execution the following morning. Joanna Gerrits asked to see him, but the mayor would not allow it, so she asked me to arrange it with her father. I said that it was not my place to meddle in the affairs of a father and daughter, and she became annoyed at me. I did not know that young ladies could spit like that. Her father apologised to me and ordered her taken home.

As compensation for his imprisonment, Jaco was given Wolf's pig, which seemed rather ironic to me. The rest of Wolf's pitiful collection of property was sold at auction and the proceeds given to the poor. The house itself stood empty for a while, then the widow De Boer leased the land and invited Gerrit Hoet to live there. I discovered all this when he came to find me one market day in Leiden and introduced me to his new fiancée, a young woman from Leiderdorp who obviously looked more comely to him than she did to me; but looks are not everything.

As I trudged back to Leiden, I felt depressed and guilty. Guilty, because a young man had died due to me. I know I did not wield the dagger, and you can argue that he brought it upon himself, but it was still a waste of two lives, his and his father's. As for Franciscus Wolf, we must believe that he received his due sentence at the hands of an Infallible Judge.

Bartholomeus de Jong visited Joost in his cell on the night before his execution. For obvious reasons, he did not discuss what was said then when he visited me the next time he came to the University library, but he said that on the morning Joost accepted his fate as the consequence of choices he had made. They prayed together, and then Joost walked firmly out to the hanging tree.

Joanna Gerrits was not at her window.

A NOTE TO THE READER

Dear Reader,

I am, as always, grateful to you for reading this far. If you have enjoyed this book, please tell your friends; if not, please keep your opinions to yourself.

In my first book Mercurius busied himself in helping ordinary people. After a couple of escapades working for the Stadhouder, it was time to bring him back to his original conception of service.

The Pesthuis, or Plague House, is a real place. I originally wanted it to play a bigger part in the story, but as it unfolded it became just a landmark. Oegstgeest is also a real place, now connected by the expansion of Leiden, but in 1680 it was a separate village.

Mercurius takes religion very seriously. He was ordained Deacon in Troyes and later Priest in Namur, and it pains him to keep his ordination secret. While there was no persecution of Catholics in his age, he was not to know that those days would not return, so one can understand his reticence in these stories, although by the time he dictates them he can feel confident enough in his safety to disclose his secret.

I have been surprised — in a good sense — by the kind way in which readers have received Master Mercurius. As reviewers note, his heart is in the right place. A few have questioned whether men in the seventeenth century were really as squeamish about capital punishment as Mercurius is, or shared his other apparently modern ideas, to which I reply that in any age people have a range of views and Mercurius would certainly not have been unique in thinking as he does.

I am particularly touched by the generous remarks of Dutch readers, who have accepted Mercurius as one of their own. Mercurius is very proud to be a Dutchman and even more so to work for the University of Leiden. I would be too.

If you have enjoyed this novel, I'd be really grateful if you would leave a review on **Amazon** and **Goodreads**. I love to hear from readers, so please keep in touch through **Facebook** or **Twitter**, or leave a message on my **website**.

Dank je wel!

Graham Brack

Sapere Books is an exciting new publisher of brilliant fiction and popular history.

To find out more about our latest releases and our monthly bargain books visit our website:
saperebooks.com

Made in United States
North Haven, CT
08 July 2023

38730749R00124